WHIMS OF THE NIGHT WINDS

A Horror Collection

by P.L. McMillan

www.saltheartpress.com

Front & back cover image by P.L. McMillan.
Book design by Molly Halstead.
Formatting by Molly Halstead.
Interior illustrations by P.L. McMillan.

First printing edition 2026.
ISBN: 979-8-9925900-9-8

Whims of the Night Winds

A Horror Collection
by P.L. McMillan

Dedicated to my cherished support system:
Agatha, Sabrina, Spuds
Deb, Chris, Julia, Tara, Tanner

Contents

A Letter from PLM

Hey there, spooky reader!

Welcome to my second collection of my horror fiction! Originally this project started out as just a little idea to collect all the stories I had written for my October Writing Challenge – a challenge I do every year, writing a story a day for seven days leading up to Halloween, based on reader submitted prompts (I added those prompts to the back of this collection, in case you're curious!).

A lot of the challenge stories really pushed me to think outside of the box, to create stories I would have never otherwise, so I am really proud of them. Some of them are bizarre, some of them are melancholy, some of them showcase my humour – all of them are pure PLM. A reflection of my writing when I'm put under pressure, no time to have second thoughts or hesitations as the midnight deadline loomed each day.

When I collected all my favourites, I saw that most of the stories were pretty short. I wanted a chunky collection, a thick collection, a collection with girth. So I decided to add some previously published work that hasn't been available outside their original anthologies.

Like "Falling", which was my very first published story and marked my first step as a proper author! It was an amazing moment to receive that token payment. Maybe it wasn't a lot of money, but it was a step forward. My first payment for my fiction. It was validation.

Or "The Rathwick Ritual on Sentinel Hill", a Lovecraftian folk horror tale, which was only available in audio form from NoSleep Podcast. Until now!

Also "Left Behind", an urban legend inspired ghost story, which was the very first story I did a live reading for (I was shaking the whole time). Huge call out to author Angela Sylvaine who gave me courage and cough drops!

To add to all these stories, I also created an epistolary story using different document formats and linocut prints I created for it. I had such a great time creating the mixed media tale, for a story idea I'd been mulling over for years. It's finally found life.

The night winds are waiting, dear reader. Can you hear them? Let's see where they lead.

x P.L. McMillan

The Widow's Walk

"I'm sorry, Mrs. Hughes." Mr. Sullivan, the town's butcher, didn't actually look sorry. Just uncomfortable. "This'll be the last I can deliver 'til you pay your tab."

Henrietta tightened her clasped hands, letting her nails bite into her palms. "Sir, you know my husband will make right just as soon as he's back."

The butcher sucked his teeth, shifting uncomfortably as he glanced over his shoulder at the crashing gray sea visible past the cliff's edge. Today the sky was as colourless as the water, both merged seamlessly at the horizon creating a dizzying illusion of a heaven-high wave.

"Happy to start deliveries again." He wouldn't look at her. "Once the tab's paid, ma'am."

Mr. Sullivan held out the small crate he carried and she took it. Normally a servant would receive the deliveries but there were none. The last of them had left two weeks ago when Henrietta had let them know she couldn't afford their pay.

Her husband had been gone for nearly a year now.

The crate felt woefully light.

She watched the butcher pull himself up to the front of his wagon—the new one that her husband had gotten for Mr. Sullivan when his old one had broken down—clicking his tongue at his chestnut nag, and left without a look back.

Henrietta opened the narrow door that stood between the bay windows in her bedroom. A walkway extended out, surrounded by pretty white railings. She knew people called them widow's walks. Places where forgotten women haunted, waiting for their loves to return.

She walked down, standing at the end, peering out at the ocean. Vicious waves crashed against the side of the cliff with resounding thunder. Henrietta could feel the salt spray on her face even where she stood.

Above, the clouds remained heavy and constant, hanging low over the land like a shroud. The sun had drowned long ago. It had been weeks since Henrietta had last felt sunshine on her face.

Her belly rumbled with hunger.

Lying in bed, Henrietta watched the ceiling. The lighthouse's cold light swept across it at regular intervals, creating deep arching shadows that then disappeared.

She rolled to her side, reached out, and brought her husband's pillow to her chest. Squeezing it tight, she buried her face in it, but his smell was gone. Long gone.

Antony was supposed to have returned long ago. Owner of the Horizon Shipping Company, Antony's business had helped the town through so many hard times—providing jobs, boosting businesses. A sailor at heart, he often went on shorter trips. To network, shake hands, make connections—that's what he'd called it.

The year had been bad for storms. Henrietta had begged him not to go.

"Wait for me, my love," he'd said. "I promise, after this, I'll return and settle."

"What if you don't return? With the storms—"

"Death himself could not keep me from you," he'd said. "My love for you would drink the oceans and swallow the sky."

"I understand your...troubles, Mrs. Hughes," Mr. Doyle, the banker, said, nodding vigorously. "But it wouldn't be fair to keep... adding to your debt without further payment in sight. What would my other clients think?"

Henrietta looked down at his hands, covered in gold rings and gems. "Sir, you know that my husband will return your kindness ten-fold if you would just—"

"Have you thought of...selling some things?" he interrupted. "At least to tide yourself over until...your husband returns?"

She nodded, though there was nothing of value to sell anymore.

"Or perhaps...seek alms from the Church?" Mr. Doyle cleared his throat, bowed, and retreated through the thin fog back to his horse.

Standing at the end of her widow's walk, Henrietta scanned the sea for the Brisk Runner. She knew what the townspeople thought.

Beneath her, the land was swathed in fog. It crept about like eels. From where she stood, Henrietta couldn't see the road, the town, or even her back garden. Only the sea and a hazy horizon sliced open by the lighthouse's beacon.

"Come back to me, Antony," she cried. "You promised!"

The house creaked in the night and Henrietta opened her eyes with a shiver. Her husband's pillow was wet with tears, crushed against her face.

In the brief illumination from the lighthouse's beam, she saw fog curling across the floor.

The door to her widow's walk was open, she could taste the sea on her lips.

The night wind gusted in and out through the door, tossing the curtains, making loose papers dance across the room, filling the halls and rooms like deep, calm breaths.

Henrietta got up, feeling dizzy. She went to the door and looked out.

The waves crashed loudly against the cliff wall and the night was dark, so dark.

She shut the door and returned to her empty bed.

"We've not much to spare, I'm afraid," Father Reed said, handing over a basket of tomatoes. "It's been a bad year for everyone."

Henrietta took the basket, stared at the priest's new leather shoes.

"We are praying for you and Mr. Hughes every Sunday," Father Reed said. "You should try and attend a service. God provides."

She didn't bother to reply.

He cleared his throat, looked out at the sea. "They say the storm of a century is coming. Be safe, my child."

Henrietta watched the priest mount his horse and gallop away, as if afraid she would chase him down. The fog was thicker now and swallowed the thin man up instantly.

Something towered in the fog, in the water. Taller than the lighthouse, taller than anything Henrietta had ever seen before. It was miles out, where the ocean would be deep. It did not move with the waves. It stood and watched her.

Its features were obscured by the fog, which grew ever thicker each day, but its two round eyes were bright and unwavering.

Hands gripping the sea-damp railing, Henrietta waited for it to move, to disappear like a figment in the fog. She watched until the invisible sun set and doused everything in darkness.

The deep hungry ache in her belly woke her. The townspeople had been true to their word. No one had come for her in weeks. Her bones stretched her skin, her head spun when she stood too fast.

Henrietta sat up, pushing herself against the pillows.

The door was open again and fog had flooded in.

"If only I could eat the fog," she whispered, her eyes prickling with tears.

The night wind rushed in and out, sounding like Antony's deep, gentle sleep breaths. Henrietta stood, knees shaking, hands gripping the bed frame for support. She went out onto the walk and stared out at the sea.

The lighthouse flashed by, revealing the towering leviathan closer than before. The light caught the briefest angles of many limbs, the sleekness of an endless flank, the curve of a vicious tail, and glittering eyes as deep and fathomless as the ocean itself.

Warm wind rushed over Henrietta, chasing away the midnight chill. She stayed on the walk, waiting for more glimpses as the light passed by, hunger forgotten for just a little while.

The cupboards were empty, the icebox barren. Henrietta held the last crust of bread she had, stale now. She took it and a glass of water up to the widow's walk. It took a long while to ascend the stairs. She rested every third one.

Her head spun, as light as the fog that now filled every room of the house. It had taken her several hours, resting frequently, but she'd opened all the doors, all the windows, to let the fog in.

Now, hanging over the edge of the railing, Henrietta dipped her bread in the water to soften it.

She savoured the texture of the food on her tongue.

Out in the ocean, it waited, a storm raging at its back. Lightning spiked out around it, slicing sizzling wounds into the water, which had drawn away from the shore in the night. Dying fish flopped in the thousands on the newly exposed seabed. The wind howled, waiting to be released with the rain. Its eyes watched her as she slowly, resolutely, ate the last of her food.

She wasn't worried. She only needed strength for a little while longer.

The bread finished, Henrietta drank the water, catching lost crumbs on her tongue.

Fog curled up her dress, her arms, her neck, danced through her hair and caressed her cheeks.

Henrietta looked at the lurker in the fog.

"Go," she said.

The storm raged the entire night and, even through the thunder and wind, Henrietta could hear the savage rending of houses and the screams of those who had turned their backs on her.

She stayed on the widow's walk, where this last hidden reserve of strength came from she did not know, but it allowed her to watch the sun rise for the first time in months and burn away the fog.

The town was gone, now a flooded graveyard of splintered walls and shattered stone. The lighthouse was cracked in half, its beacon in shards on the beach.

The way revealed, Henrietta took the cliffside path down to the pebbly beach beneath her home.

The tide was low, crabs raced by with claws full of fish flesh.

There, tucked under the cliff, was the battered, barnacle-encrusted hull of the Brisk Runner. For as he had promised, Antony had returned to her and, in the golden light of the reborn sun, Henrietta laid herself down on the broken shell of her husband's ship and died.

Lens Obscura

"There's nothing wrong with the contacts."

"I'm seeing things I shouldn't," I reply.

He only shakes his head. I slip the tech back on. The system syncs to my brain. In my peripherals, I see alerts about the weather, texts from my mother, an ad for a sale. I step outside the shop and she's waiting in the dusk. She smiles with her sharp, shark's teeth. People walk through her, but that doesn't stop her from being there. I remove the contacts. She's gone. The world is blurry, I'll have to stumble home. She's gone, but I know she's waiting.

Mistress Edge's House of Horrors

It was a typical cheesy haunted house—white paint flaking off the sides, boarded-up windows, and rotting rose trellises. The building was a two-storied Victorian affair complete with a widow's walk, despite there being no sea or even river nearby. The large French doors that led inside had been thrown open and were framed by two large bay windows. Cotton cobwebs and fake police tape had been strewn liberally about the railings.

The only recent edition was a neon, burlesque-style sign that blinked out the words "Mistress Edge's House of Horrors." Eerie organ music crept from the century-old windows and I could see strobe lights flashing in some of the rooms.

It was only half past seven so the sky was still light with a washed-out evening sun. Long, thin shadows draped over the house, the cracked sidewalk, and the two dozen people waiting in line. The properties next to the old house were empty, weed-infested lots, so the line was able to stretch into the one on the right. The lot on the left was a third full with the cars belonging to the individuals in line.

Kyle Porter made his way back to me from the middle of the street where he'd been taking panorama shots of the house and surrounding area, as well as the excited faces of those in line. He bounced the camera in his palm.

"Got two panoramas and some close-ups of the decorations. Wanna get your intro done while we wait?" he asked.

"Here?" I looked around me.

The other people in line were looking up at the house, but I knew I would get attention by reeling out a spiel to a camera.

"Why not?" Kyle cocked an eyebrow.

He was a stupidly handsome man who knew how good-looking he was, which only served to make him more insufferable. He had never made it through college, just picked up a quarter of a degree in cinematography. Angela Burges didn't care though; he took decent enough shots and was happy to be paid below the industry standard. His blond hair was artfully tussled, cleft chin and defined jaw covered in just enough stubble to make him look like he didn't care how he looked.

Of course, I could dig at him for his quarter of a degree, but I got my degree in journalism and here I was, six years older than him and doing a fluff piece on a haunted house. Not only that, but it was my first real exposure piece. I had only written meaningless regurgitation articles needed to boost the website's traffic, pieces that said nothing in 500 words or less. This was the first real article Angela had assigned to me. I didn't even know where to start. I wasn't used to being in front of a camera, but Angela wanted a first-person view of the experience with commentary. I felt completely out of my comfort zone, but I didn't want douchebag Kyle to know that.

"Let's wait until after. That way I can use the experience to tailor my opening a bit."

He shrugged and took out his phone. He became absorbed in whatever it was he was looking at, so I took my time examining the other people in line. I pulled a notepad and pen from my purse, in case

I wanted to jot down notes about any standouts. For this advanced screening, I had assumed that most would be journalists, bloggers, and podcasters. Everyone seemed to fit this assumption, except for the group standing directly in front of me in line. These four were dressed in corsets, tight pleather pants, mesh shirts, and lacy skirts that barely covered anything. The two women had thick eyeliner, multiple pierced ears, and neon streaked hair. The two men had gel-spiked hair, eyeliner, and facial piercings.

I noted down their appearance and wondered at what the group was doing here. This was supposed to be a press release review, open only to those publications and websites famous enough to be liable to generate the reviews the company wanted for their new business venture.

Kyle was still engrossed in his phone. I leaned in and saw he was furiously swiping right on every girl that popped up on whatever dating app he was currently on. My curiosity got the best of me, so I shrugged past him, closer to the darkly dressed foursome.

"Excuse me?" I started.

The four were bent over a book. It looked like a biography. On the cover was a large black-and-white picture of an older woman dressed in Victorian-era clothing, a slight smile on her face.

"Hello!" I tried again.

I caught the attention of one of the women, the one with a violent purple streak marking the left side of her hair. She turned to me and gave me the once-over.

"Hello, I was hoping to ask you some questions?" I hated how hesitant my voice was. Angela wouldn't be so timid, she would have burst into the group and taken over the conversation, guiding it the way that would be most advantageous to her article.

The other three had turned to me. I felt their gazes heavy on my face.

"Ah, yes. I'm Katy Marshall, writer for The Net Gazette," I swallowed hard. "I noticed that you don't seem to be part of the journalist crowd and was wondering about how you got invited?"

Even to me, my question sounded insulting. Like they didn't belong.

The man with the double eyebrow piercings, black hair, and mesh tank top grinned at me. His smile was wide, dazzling white, and welcoming.

"For sure! I'm Charles, this is Amanda," he nodded at the purple-haired girl with the ultra-tight lacey corset and bulging breasts.

He gestured to the man who stood beside him, who was clad in a black pleather vest over a pin-striped button up and tight pleather pants that jangled with heavy chains.

"Kirk."

This left the woman wearing the skin-tight crimson dress with a black under-bust that exaggerated her tiny breasts. Complimenting her outfit was a large skull tattoo that covered most of her left shoulder and arm. Her face was tinted with makeup to resemble a ghostly hue, her eyes darkened with black eyeshadow, and her brows artificially lengthened with brow pencil.

"And my girlfriend, Bee."

I nodded and shook each of their hands.

"This is Kyle, my cameraman."

Kyle looked up from his phone and gave the women a head-to-toe examination with a wry grin. They stared back at him, unimpressed by his pastel polo shirt and designer jeans.

"Are you four part of a podcast, or?" I led them on.

"Us? No, not at all," Charles said.

Kirk painfully squeezed his hand into the right-hand ass pocket of his pleather pants, pulling out a crumpled pamphlet. He offered it to me with a shy smile. Taking it, I read the words "Mistress Constance Edge —expert in Egyptian history and talented poetess" in Gothic lettering. Underneath was the very same picture I glimpsed in the book they'd been peering at. When I opened the pamphlet, I saw someone's enthusiastic attempt at making it read like a newspaper from the 1800s. At least seven fonts had been used, interchanged with black-and-white pictures of the woman, her house, the pyramids, and a scarab.

On the left-hand side was a poem, leaning crooked against the margin.

"From death's grip, I take you back,
Frothing, twisting,
Wet with a rotting placenta,
I smell the scent of the afterlife,
A dank, dark musk of underground things,
You're back, you're back,
Blood, bone, skin, but empty –
I am not God, not omnipotent, not infallible,
I'll take you as you are now,
Take me as I am and forgive me my flaws."

The middle had a short biography underneath a cameo of Mistress Constance Edge herself.

"Born 1910, died 1989. Mistress Edge (maiden name Crowell) was a self-professed female explorer and poetess. She became enamored with Egyptian culture after the famous discovery of Tutankhamun in 1922 and studied everything she could. After her marriage to Colonel Richard Edge at the age of 18, she joined him on his many trips to Egypt. On their trips to Cairo, Mistress Edge collected artifacts and the local legends—spending more time with the natives than her husband cared for. She tried many times to get her collection of folklore and stories published but was rejected due to her gender.

She took to writing the dark, Gothic poems so many love to this very day—publishing them under a pseudonym (Christopher Patterson). Her husband died four years after their wedding, without giving her a child. Unable to travel on her own as a woman, Mistress Edge returned to the family home.

Her fortune being rather well-known, Mistress Edge had many suitors but none that lasted. Most ghosted after courting her for however many months. The social circles gossiped she was too "peculiar" to wed again. She died alone, in 1989."

On the right-hand side was a hand-drawn ankh and the words: "Pamphlet produced by the Edge Society. Est. 2002."

I closed the pamphlet and examined Mistress Edge's photograph again. She looked to be about forty, though the harsh sun of Cairo could have aged her prematurely. Despite the fuzziness of the old photograph, it was clear to see her skin was dark, weathered, and lined. Even so, her eyes were bright, her smile alluring. She was dressed in a tight, striped dress with a scarab-shaped pin at her throat.

I offered the pamphlet back.

"Nah, keep it!" Kirk said.

"So, you guys are part of the Edge Society?" I tucked the paper into my purse.

Kyle took a step back, camera rolling in his hands.

"We *are* the Edge Society. The founding four. We have about thirty subscribers though. We put out a poetry anthology based on her work. I was the editor," Bee said.

"Oh, that's cool. What was it called?"

Angela loved characters, so she would definitely get a kick out of this group. It could add a more personal touch to the piece as well.

"The Gothic Edge." Bee whipped out her phone and pulled up an image on the screen.

Kyle obliged by zooming in, taking a few seconds to record the black-and-white cover crowded with black roses, more ankhs, and a low, sickly moon.

"I didn't realize this haunted house had such a rich history. But if you're not with a website or podcast, how did you get an invite?" I asked.

"Bee's cousin is banging the guy who is running this," Amanda smirked.

"We couldn't pass up a chance to see the inside of Constance's house. All the original stuff is gone, of course, sold in auctions or donated to the museum here in town. It will be amazing to see the inside all the same," Charles said.

"Did you hear anything about how they've decorated it then?" I was drawing a blank on questions.

Angela would have been pulling out gems left, right, and center. Kyle looked bored out of his mind and I was fairly sure I saw him zoom in on Amanda's chest. I resisted the urge to elbow him.

"My cousin said they went for the basic haunted house package, I'm sure it's going to be completely lame. They're more leaning on the house's reputation to bring in people than their abysmal theme choice," Bee said, sticking a clove cigarette between her lips.

"How would you have designed it then?" I asked.

Charles, Amanda, and Kirk all looked at Bee. It was obvious she was the leader of the "Society," probably the anthology was her idea as a way to get her own writing out into the world on the back of Constance Edge's. The Queen Bee. I smiled to myself as the Queen herself sucked at her cigarette. Then she looked at the camera and smiled. Her smile brightened up her whole face, making her gorgeous.

"Obviously, I would capitalize on Constance's obsession with the occult and Egyptian mythology. I'd lay heavy on the curse of the Pharaoh. People talked, you know, they thought a curse followed her back from Cairo. That a curse killed her husband because she was taking so many artifacts from the tombs. You can find old diaries and family logs in the town's library and nearly all of them say so. I'd copy those entries and hand them out to the people in line, really stir up the anticipation.

"Even after Colonel Edge died, she kept all the artifacts and even had her husband's old friends ship her more. Everyone thought that the curse was to blame for her loneliness too. That it chased her suitors away and eventually drove her mad. Her poems, which I would make sure were posted on the walls inside, clearly showed her descent into senility. She went from grieving her husband to believing he was still with her, to mourning the fact she was alone, before going on about how life wasn't worth living without companionship.

"I'd carry on that theme in the house—all black, dark, thick velvet, and symbolism. Create the fear of death and hopelessness in the people, not cheap thrills." Bee smirked, dropping her cigarette butt onto the sidewalk, and grinding the heel of one carefully scuffed boot on it.

"Scare them through hopelessness?" I had never heard anything stupider.

Bee nodded. Night was falling quickly now, the streetlights clicked on and cast a sickly pallor on everyone waiting. The strobe lights in the house were more noticeable and jarring. Before I could tell him to, Kyle took some video of the night-stained building. At that moment, ethereal green spotlights lit up the front of the house, and the boom of thunder echoed out from hidden speakers.

A woman dressed as Constance Edge stepped out from inside the house, her face a ghastly white and her eyes completely black. She waved at the crowd and all around me, everyone cheered.

"Welcome my ghouls and ghosts!" Faux Mistress Edge said, her voice caught by the microphone in her hand.

Bee looked at me and rolled her eyes.

"I am your hostess, Mistress Constance Edge, and this is my house of horrors!" There was a well-timed clatter at the windows as costumed employees inside the house pounded on them. "As you can see, my other guests are restless, so let's not keep them waiting!"

The crowd cheered again.

"I know you've been waiting eagerly, but due to city ordinances, I can only host ten of you at a time. So, let's get the first unlucky ten inside!"

The crowd cheered again. I went onto my tiptoes and counted. I was number nine, just making it into the first round. I was glad for this, I wanted nothing more than to get this dumb thing over with so I could go hit up a bar.

The line began to shift forward. Faux Edge greeted each and every guest with a curtsy. Kyle remained diligent and filmed the whole thing.

"Welcome, my dears," Faux Edge said to the camera, curtsying even deeper.

I slipped inside after the Edge Society. I found myself in the foyer, lit by a dim red light cast by small fake candles mounted on the walls. It was a large room, accommodating all ten of us. Faux Edge followed Kyle in, closing the door behind her and taking her place as our tour guide at the head of the group.

I started as someone ran across the length of the room above us, their pounding steps shaking dust from the ceiling. From somewhere deeper into the house, someone cackled. I took in the decorations—secondhand shop scenic prints on the walls, a cracked side table off to the left held a plastic skull, and the ceiling was heavy with more cotton cobwebs. A fuzzy stuffed black widow spider had been fastened where the overhead chandelier should have been. The floor was bare, damaged hardwood marked with glow-in-the-dark runners to guide the way through the house.

"Follow me, my dears. I'll give you the tour of a deathtime," Faux Edge cackled and made her way to the back of the house, along the path of the glow-in-the-dark strips.

"This is lame as shit, I knew it," the Queen Bee whispered in my ear.

The next room was a long, musty hall lit by more fake candles. The double French doors off to the right had been nailed shut to deter wayward explorers. As our group of ten passed a small closet, the door burst open. Several people screamed as an employee dressed in a skeleton costume jumped out at us. Though I had been expecting cheap thrills, I still started, cringing back against Kyle.

"Watch the camera!" he said.

Around me, everyone laughed off their fright.

"What can I say? I have skeletons in my closet!" Faux Edge said.

Most of the guests laughed. Bee was keeping at my side for who knew what reason. Maybe she thought I'd write about her anthology or the Edge Society and give it some publicity.

"Stupid," she hissed in my ear. "I was expecting this to be bad, but not this awful. You can trust that I'll be writing them a bad review on Yelp. I'm sure you'll mention how overly disrespectful this whole thing is in your blog."

"Website," I muttered under my breath. But really, on the internet, wasn't it all the same? The only thing that made a difference was ad revenue.

Faux Edge drew us on. We went through the dark hallway and were guided into a dining room on the right, through another set of French doors. I heard some of those ahead of me screaming as someone or something scared them. Kyle pushed past me, holding the camera up and trying to get a good shot. Expecting the jump scare, I didn't even flinch when the two men dressed in fluorescent rags lunged out at me. The room was decked out with a half dozen different coloured strobe lights—I wondered if I should put in a trigger warning for any epileptics that might be interested in going to this attraction.

Four slim girls dressed as Victorian dolls lurched around the perimeter of the room, giggling, and making clawing motions at the nearby guests. All in all, it was shaping up to be your typical haunted house. Past the dining room was the kitchen, complete with zombie chef and butler, and up the servant stairs to the second-story bedroom where a demon woman writhed on a four-poster bed with a duo of masked cultists chanting around the bedside. I soon came to expect the jump scares—from inside the kitchen closet, under the bed, from behind doors and curtains—so I made notes in my notepad and watched everyone else react.

Bee accosted me again in the bedroom. She seemed determined to give me her own version of a specialized tour. We stood at the back of the crowd while Faux Edge went on about how she was a scream in bed (the bound girl gave an obliging shriek for her joke.)

"I managed to find an obscure diary in the town's library. It had been donated by the Hawthorne family and written by a great-great aunt of theirs who had worked at the family pharmacy. In one of her entries, on July 2nd, 1935, she mentioned receiving a sealed courier message from Mistress Edge. Judith Hawthorne, that was the great-great aunt, didn't go into details. Just that she went to this house to "administer emergency services" and gave Mistress Edge a couple doses of opiates for any residual pain. Judith wrote another entry, a week later, saying she went back to the house to check up on the widow but was turned away at the door."

I automatically made notes in my notepad but was only half listening to her over the actors' screeches and chanting.

"But I dug deeper. Why didn't Mistress Edge go to the doctor? Why did she need emergency procedures at home? So, I asked some of the residents at the retirement home and found a couple people who remembered the old spinster, Judith Hawthorne. They said Judith could never get a husband because she wasn't respectable. They said she wasn't respectable because she often did back-door abortions or secret deliveries for unmarried women. She would steal supplies from the pharmacy and even visit women in different nearby towns," Bee said, watching me as I wrote down her story into my notepad. "I made a timeline. Her lover during that period was reported to be a travelling bible seller, Patrick O'Hara. The records and old timers had all agreed he left town in November the previous year, having stayed a month. He just up and left, didn't even pay for the last week he stayed at the local hotel. A retired maid told me that he'd even left his box of bibles behind, he must have been in quite the rush to get out of here. I think he got her preggo and ditched. She didn't leave the house much so no one would have noticed her belly swelling. The baby must have died in childbirth because no one had ever mentioned it and I couldn't find any records of an abandoned child. Maybe she buried it in the backyard or something!"

I stared at the bed, looking past the actors, and tried to imagine that poor woman all alone, struggling through the pain of childbirth in secret, only to have a dead child in her arms. I pitied her. I couldn't blame her for writing such dark and lonely poetry. Great, I was in a haunted house attraction, and I felt more sad than scared.

Bee's eyes were twinkling, or maybe it was the strobe light. It was obvious she was proud of all the information she'd gathered, all the secrets she had dug up—if it were all true of course. It could make a good scandal sidebar for my video if Angela would allow the speculation.

We toured through two more bedrooms, a study, and a bathroom—where voodoo priestesses, zombies, crazed lunatics, and more Victorian doll ladies waited—until we were led down the main stairs descending to the landing. Thousands of glow-in-the-dark streamers hung from the ceiling, vibrant in the black light. The landing contained the entrance to a second set of stairs descending into the basement, all the other doors leading to the rest of the house had been boarded up.

I couldn't suppress a shudder. The tour obviously ended in the basement. Bee pushed past Kyle to lean into my ear. Faux Edge went on and on, layering on a heavy coating of puns and corny jokes.

"I can't believe it! I didn't think they'd let us in the basement—but this is amazing. That's where they found her, Mistress Edge, I mean. She was dead in the basement for a week before the milkman called the police when he saw that she wasn't collecting the milk. They busted down the door and searched the house. The police found her in the basement, where she kept her most prized Egyptian relics." Bee's breath was hot and sour on my face, she was panting with excitement. "She'd lost it at the end. Completely bat-shit crazy. After her last lover, a Mr. Roger Bartholomew, disappeared, she completely secluded herself. Widowed, abandoned three times by lovers, she couldn't deal with it. They say she drank laudanum. The poison made her delusional and she crawled to the basement, she took down her hooks and palm wine, her balsam saps and tree resin, and her yards and yards of linen. And she tried to mummify herself. Straight up tried to mummify herself. She died having wrapped herself up to her waist in resin and linen."

Her lips brushed against my earlobe, oddly sensual, and I shuddered again. The group was going down the narrow wooden steps, one at a time. Bee slipped in ahead of Kyle, grabbing hold of Charles's hand. I realized I was shivering. I was the last one on the landing, looking down the purple-lit stairwell. The lights were set to a low pulse, causing the shadows to throb across the walls. The guests' silhouettes were grotesque ghouls dancing against the stone. Kyle poked his head around the corner and looked up at me. He was laughing—or grimacing.

I forced myself to descend. Even over the low, deep bass-heavy music piping in through some hidden speakers, I could hear the old wooden stairs creaking under my weight. I pictured myself plunging downward as one collapsed, of being impaled on the splintered wood. I hopped down to the floor from the third last step, my heart thudding in my ears.

The basement was huge, the width and length of the house. The floor was packed dirt, its walls rough stones. At the other end, where it would open onto the side yard of the house, was an upward opening door. A bright exit sign had been affixed above it and the glow-in-the-dark guidance strips led right to it. Black fabric had been hung from hooks in the ceiling, along with black lights, and foam body parts that swung gently. A smoke machine hidden somewhere in the shadows spewed out trails of chilly smoke that caught up around my ankles and swirled up my calves. Metal shelves had been bolted to the walls. On the shelves were plastic skulls with light-up eyes, sealed jars with prop hearts, eyeballs, brains, and toy rats. On others were books, hooks, knives, and tiny replicas of the pyramids.

In the corner, directly across from the stairs, and lit up with a ghastly green light, was a life-size sarcophagus propped up against the wall. I could faintly see three or four more spread out along the length of the room – I could only assume that actors were waiting inside, intent on scaring the guests.

"Welcome to my last and most important room, my basement laboratory. Where I practiced my dark arts, learned from Egyptian priests in the sands of Cairo," Faux Edge cried, spreading her arms wide.

I slid more toward the right, towards the exit, to get a better view of the finale. Perhaps, as well, to be closer to the exit. Kyle was multi-tasking, holding the camera above the heads of the other guests while also typing away on his phone. The air down in the basement was heavy, damp, cold, and thick with the smell of mildew.

"I was obsessed with dark arts, you see. All alone in my house, struck with a gloomy disposition, I was drawn to evil and it to me!" Our host ran a hand down the side of the sarcophagus, slowly, seductively.

Bee looked over her shoulder at me. I couldn't see her face clearly, but I could only assume that she was rolling her eyes or making a sour face.

"During my last years on this earth, I craved power, craved immortality. There's nothing more immortal than living on, preserved in resin and linen, forever and perfect. Look at my poetry and you'll see, hear, taste my madness. I put my words of power in those poems. Listen, listen to the very last poem written—found in this very house, written in blood on a scrap of paper clutched in my hand. The policeman who found it, kept it. His grandson then sold it online for quite the penny to the very same man who has brought my house back to life around you."

I saw Bee perk up. She stood on her tiptoes, hand on Charles' shoulder, trying to see over the heads of everyone else. The other members of the Edge Society whispered to each other, pulled out phones, started filming.

"Repeat after me, my ghoulish friends, so that we can maximize our power in this hallowed place of mine," said Faux Edge.

I sighed, knowing a finale when I heard one. I could guess that the actors' cue was when we finished the poem and I could only hope it was a short one.

"Anubis, I channel you!" she began, and the guests repeated her words back.

"Great and dark is your touch!"

I listened to everyone chanting along. With the shadows cloaking them, everyone looked like cult members, praying to some dark demon. I could see that even Kyle was mouthing along, a grin on his cookie-cutter beautiful face. I thought about writing down the words of the poem to put in my piece, but figured the video would be good enough.

"See my skin and bones and flesh,
Weigh my heart and soul and mind,
Find me worthy, find me your willing supplicant."

I thought about Constance Edge, down here in the dark, wrapping herself with linen and resin. Lost in the fog of the poison she'd ingested, driven to suicide by her lonely life. She'd found comfort in Egyptian mythology, it'd brought something more to her life, even though it couldn't save her from herself in the end.

"Raise me up in your arms,
Bring me up!
Raise me, raise me,
Save me, save me."

I jumped when I felt a hand on my arm. Who else but Bee, standing by my side again.

"I can't believe this! I was the last bidder for that poem until some anonymous buyer got it last minute. Now they're using it as some sick prop for their haunted house when it should be cherished for the treasure it is. I am so furious! You need to share this in your newspaper, really rip into them for shitting on Constance's memory like this," she said, not caring that she was talking over Faux Edge.

"This doesn't sound like a poem."

"Osiris, I channel you!"

"That's because it's not, not really. The last year of her life, Constance didn't publish any more poems, she didn't even really write them. She wrote papers on Egyptian funerary rites and their idea of the afterlife. She was so fanatical; she thought their gods were real and had the power to grant rebirth to their most loyal followers. In one of her papers displayed in the town museum, she claimed to have written a prayer she knew would work," Bee said. "This must have been that prayer!"

"Hot and searing burns your gaze,
See my intentions, pure and true,
See my devotion, unwavering."

"So, she wanted to die and come back to life? To a life she hated enough to kill herself?" I asked.

I felt Bee shrug, her shoulder brushing against mine.

"Weigh my worth,
Weigh me true.
Let me pass,
Let me pass beyond the gates of death."

"It doesn't really make sense, I agree. Did you feel that?" Bee asked.

I looked at her. She was peering down at the ground. I looked down between my feet and saw nothing.

"It felt like a mini-earthquake or something," she said.

"Let me pass, let me pass!
Let me pass beyond the gates of death!" the chanters finished.

Underneath my flats, I felt a small tremor. Panicked thoughts ran through my head, images of an earthquake hitting the house and it crashing down on us. I pictured myself being crushed by the heavy wooden beams above me or under the sheer weight of rubble.

I took a step toward the cellar storm door. I hesitated. I couldn't see clearly through the darkness and the fake fog, but the hard-packed dirt floor was cracking, heaving upwards in dry chunks. It was the vibrations of the earth moving that I felt under the thin soles of my shoes. Underneath the music and the laughter of the guests, I could hear the dry dirt being pushed up.

"Bee, Bee, look," I reached back blindly, trying to grab her arm.

Was this some elaborate hoax, the big twist at the end of the tour, the showstopper?

Bee's thin, cold hand gripped mine tightly, painfully so. She pulled me back, away from the exit, and clutched at my shoulder with her other hand, hiding behind me.

"Shit, what is that? What *is* that?" she said, her voice high-pitched in my ear.

"Part of the show, maybe there are trapdoors under the dirt," I said.

I heard several screams and spun around. A scantily clad woman, dressed in an Egyptian themed skirt and bikini top, eyes lined thickly with black had jumped out of the closest sarcophagus. More actors must be waiting, under the ground in trapdoors and in the others, I reassured myself.

I looked toward the exit, so close, just across the dirt floor that was cracking open. Three pale figures were pulling themselves out of the ground. They were wrapped tightly in linen strips, stained by the dirt that had acted as their coffins.

Bee's nails dug into my shoulder and hand, she stumbled back against the wall, pulling me with her. Faux Edge gestured toward the exit, a coy smile on her face. Everyone else turned and began to make their way towards it, brushing past the draped fabric and fake body parts. The mummies stood, broad shouldered and of varying heights. Beyond them, a smaller figure struggled against the dirt. Its infant limbs were swaddled in the dirty linen as well, its tiny head flopped weakly on the floor.

"Oh, that's sick! Sick, so sick," Bee was whimpering.

One of the other guests pointed at the mummies, laughed, and half turned towards the rest of the group. The mummies swayed on their feet. One reached out and clawed at the fabric wrapped around its face, scratching at it.

"We should leave, we should run past them," I said. "We need to get out of here."

I wondered how much shit Kyle would give me for panicking and bolting out of this lame haunted house. I wondered if Angela would ever be able to take me seriously when he told her how I had fled. I faltered, took a step, stopped.

Faux Edge had stopped too, her hands up to her face. Her back was to me, but I watched her shoulders tense, I saw her take a step back. She reached out to the group as they went on.

"Charles!" Bee screamed.

Her boyfriend was stepping past the first mummy. At the sound of her voice, he looked over his shoulder. The mummy reached up and grabbed the thin boy's throat, lifting him up towards the ceiling.

"Charles, no!"

This time it was me restraining her, pulling her back. I heard the crack of Charles' neck over the music. His body dropped. The mummies lunged. It was chaos. I couldn't think over the screaming.

Three more bodies dropped.

The actors in the sarcophaguses had stepped out, drawn by the noise. Kyle turned—I saw the gaping hole of his screaming mouth. I saw the mummy grabbing him by his shoulders, the linen around its mouth stretching and ripping as it opened its jaw and sunk yellowed teeth into his neck, staining its linen red.

The other guests floundered in the hanging fabric, some fell over as their legs became twisted, others trampled those on the ground in their attempt to flee. Faux Edge shoved past me screaming, I fell against Bee, we tumbled to the floor. Our host left us there, I heard her screams echoing through the first-floor rooms as she fled.

"It's them, it's her lovers!" Bee was crying into my hair.

The three mummies had the last three victims in their arms, biting into their flesh and breaking their bones. Kyle clutched his neck, trying to drag himself away from the monsters with his free hand. He was mouthing something at us, at me, blood bubbling at his lips.

"They didn't leave town, fuck, they never left at all!"

I ignored her and stood, pulling her to her feet. The sound of us standing, our limbs scraping up against the stone wall, grabbed the dead men's attention. All three cocked their heads, listening in unison. I held my breath and prayed that Bee was too. The tallest one was holding a thin woman by the hair, she hung limp. The other two dropped their victims—another woman, this one stockier, and a young man with red hair and a face stained crimson with blood. They stood, blinded by the linen wrapped around their eyes, and listened.

My whole body was shaking and I couldn't get it under control.

I knew that if I made even the tiniest sound, they would start towards us. Kyle had stopped too, hand wrapped tightly around his own neck, head turned away from me and looking at the still mummies. Then he coughed, blood splattered across the dirt floor. He shot me a single terrified look and then the mummies were on him, tearing and clawing at his flesh.

I turned my back on his convulsing body and pulled Bee up the stairs, taking the steps two at a time. The stairs thundered with our escape and the mummies opened wide their rotten mouths, chasing us with their howls. Bee was dead weight, dragging me back, but I refused to let go. I pulled her up to the top of the stairs and through the circuitous route we had followed to get there.

"She killed them, oh fuck, she *mummified* them!" Bee sobbed.

I jerked on her arm to shut her up as we ran through the second-floor rooms. This place was a fire hazard with its boarded-up windows and doors, only two exits to speak of. The employees we'd seen on our way in were gone. They must have panicked when Faux Edge came through—panicked and left the guests behind.

"CONSTANCE!" came a gurgling roar behind us.

Against my better judgement, I looked back over my shoulder. The largest mummy had caught up, its linen splattered with blood, its mouth full of broken, yellowed teeth and a squirming, rotting tongue. It reached out for us, reached out for the woman it thought was us. The floor was gone, my left foot encountered only air, and then I was tumbling down the servants' stair to the first floor.

My head slammed against a wall and my vision blacked out. I felt myself hitting the walls, the stairs, finally coming to a bruised rest at the bottom. I felt hands on me and tried to scream, but my wind had been knocked out of me.

"Get up, you dumb bitch, get *up!*"

I was pulled to my feet, yanked away from the stairs. My vision faded back; it was now Bee leading the way. Her surprisingly strong hand gripped my wrist as we wound our way through the final rooms.

"CONSTANCE!" the mummy howled.

Somewhere upstairs, the two other mummies joined in its howl. My eardrums pounded with the sheer volume of their rising voices; it was unearthly, spectral, supernatural. In the foyer, I saw blue and red lights flashing through the windows that flanked the front doors, which had thankfully been left open.

Bee dropped my wrist, her long legs carrying her through the doorway and into safety. I lost momentum; my legs seemed made of lead as I tried to catch up. I felt a wrenching pain in my scalp as my hair became entangled in something and my legs flew out from under me as I jerked backward. Falling, I stared up at the blind face of the mummy that had caught me. Its one gnarled, clawed fist was gripping my hair while the other began to reach for my face, even as I hit the floor.

I heard two loud bouts of thunder and saw a thick, black spray erupt from the back of the mummy's head, painting the ceiling above in sludgey rotten brains. The violence of the attack threw back its head, flinging it away from me, and onto the floor—a handful of my hair with it.

I scrambled to my hands and knees, scuttling away. Rough hands hooked under my armpits, jerking me to my feet. Through tear-blurred vision, I saw a cop before he shoved me, unceremoniously, through the front door and out into safety.

Paramedics were waiting on the front lawn. Lost in the visual confusion of tears, flashing lights, and the explosion of phone camera flashes, I let myself be led to the seclusion of an ambulance. Bee was wrapped in a blanket, sitting on the fender. Her shaking fingers held a clove cigarette to her lips. I sat next to her, accepting the cigarette when she passed it to me.

Behind us, in the body of the ambulance, the paramedics fussed around gathering whatever they needed to tend to the gaping hole where some of my hair used to be. A warm trickle of blood slipped down my forehead into my eyebrow.

The cigarette smoke filled my lungs and sent a pleasant buzz to my brain. My whole body was shaking and felt completely numb.

"Sorry, uh, you know. I didn't mean to just ditch you. I wasn't thinking. Especially after you saved me," Bee said, not meeting my gaze.

I shrugged. Then flinched at the distant sound of more gunfire. I wondered if they'd shot Constance's mummy baby.

I thought of what would happen next. This was something spectacular, something horrifying, something the public would be desperate to know about so I knew I could expect police interviews, a media circus, the world's attention. I began to grin.

This was my break.

Even if it was just for a moment, I was going to be famous and, if I played this right, I could capitalize on it and make a fortune. I ducked my head down as I felt myself shaking, on the brink of giggles. Images of talk shows, interviews, maybe even a book based on my experience, flashed before my eyes. Me, the fearless reporter. Bee, my Judas. I sucked in a steadying breath. Angela had always said that audiences loved a survivor story.

"I can't blame you," I said.

I made sure my grin was gone before I looked up at Bee.

"Why don't you give me your contact details? It will be good to keep in touch."

It was only when she had entered her number into my phone then staggered away to call her parents that I buried my face in my grimy hands to stifle my elated laughter.

The Butcher of Edge Fallow

"Fuck." Joe looked down at the twisted body of the once perfect 10/10 blond jock.

The kid lay twisted at the bottom of the dried up creek, having fallen trying to escape Joe. His body was face down, his head was face up. Kid was def dead.

Joe looked down at his machete. Shiny in the moonlight. Absolutely fucking unstained by any goddamn virgin/jock/stoner/nerd/outcast goth kid blood. He sighed.

Thirteen years in a row and no real goddamn kills.

Frustrated, only hours to go before midnight this All Hallow's Eve, Joe turned and began to make his way back to Lovers' Lane. Surely there were some sexually active youths there to kill. This jock had been too fast for Joe, outrun him like this was the goddamn football field. Up until the kid had fallen head first into Dry Skull Creek.

Joe shook his head again. "What a waste."

He strode steadily through the woods, always a power walk, never a run if he could help it—running made him dizzy. His blackened dead heart couldn't keep up.

Joe thought about his predicament. Thirteen years ago, he'd been a teen at Cordel High School—Go Warthogs!—a nerd, bullied relentlessly. When Cindy, the head cheerleader, asked him to Homecoming, he'd really thought he'd been noticed. Been seen.

Instead, the football team and cheer squad had chased him from the dance with cow prods, eggs. They'd chased him through the fields and down country roads, until his heart had given out under a cold sickle moon at the crossroads of Sulphur St and Main.

The following Halloween, he'd woken. Woken with the knowledge that he could never rest until he'd wet a blade with enough blood to fill his heart again.

Up ahead, he spotted moonlight glinting off the roofs of several cars. Far enough apart that the passengers had privacy from each other.

Joe lurked in the shadows beneath the trees.

Of course, they didn't call him Joe anymore. Or Joe the Poor Shmoe as they'd mocked him in high school.

Now he was The Butcher. Joe flexed his wrist, hearing his tendons creak, his skin cracked in deep fissures that reeked of rot.

He sucked in a breath, straightened his shoulders.

The girls in the front bench seating of the nearest car were too busy necking—did they still call it that?—to notice his approach. In the fogged side window, Joe caught sight of his chosen face before he yanked open the door.

The girls screamed. He pulled out the closest one with a bit too much enthusiasm and ended up landing on his ass. The girl kicked at him, her slim legs surprisingly powerful, screams alerting the others.

Headlights turned on, blinding him. The other girl in the car kept screaming and screaming, as she slid over to the steering wheel, threw the car in reverse, and promptly ran over her girlfriend—popping out intestines and blood all over the dirt—before squealing away.

The other cars followed, leaving Joe and his non-victim, alone in the dark.

He adjusted his mask. It was the old Warthog mascot head he'd stolen his third Halloween. After he'd claimed it, it had stayed with him ever since. It made him feel more powerful. Made with real tanned pig skin bristling with black hair, a gaping thick-lipped mouth with cracked wooden tusks, a stubby scarred black snout, and deep shadowy eye holes. It covered the whole of his head. It was a good thing he didn't need to breathe anymore.

Looking up, Joe sighed. The moon was lower. Daybreak was coming and, with it, another year of purgatory. He had to kill someone with his blade, anyone.

Power walking with a purpose, Joe made his way to the local campground. Kids loved that place. Drinking, drugs, whatever. As he approached, he smelled the bonfire before he saw it. A ton of kids there, easy pickings—hopefully. Most were stumbling around, necking it on the dirt, dry humping to some ugly thumping music.

Joe lurched into the clearing, machete raised.

A kid noticed and screamed; "The Butcher!"

They stampeded. It was chaos.

Joe swung his blade, he had to hit someone at this rate—there were so many. His warthog mask slipped on his sweaty face and he missed the nearest teen by a mile.

Several of the idiots fell into the bonfire, their booze stained clothes catching instantly and setting them ablaze.

Another asshole ran straight into a sharp branch, popping his own eye, piercing his brain.

Joe grabbed someone who tried to pass him, raised his blade again. A girl shoved him and he fell onto his back. The same girl fell over him, a broken bottle impaling her straight through the mouth and out the back of her neck.

Rolling over on his belly, Joe adjusted his mask, and reached for his dropped machete.

Some gym rat with a buzz cut ran at him, axe in hand. Gripping his machete, Joe struggled to get to his knees.

"Die, you monster!" the kid yelled, his voice breaking on the last syllable, and the kid's foot rolled on a beer bottle.

Unbalanced, the boy windmilled his arms, managing to catch two others in their throats with his axe. The three went down.

"Fuck me," Joe said, frustrated. He could feel the night waning and, with it, his chance at rest, at peaceful oblivion.

He had no idea who decided he needed to "get revenge for his torments" but he didn't think it was fucking fair. Joe had been happy to finally escape his bullies, the terrible life he lived in the town of Edge Fallow. But here he fucking was, forced to chase after idiots every fucking Halloween for a chance to finally be left alone.

Blue and red lights washed over the scene. He sighed, standing with his machete.

"Put your fucking hands up!" a man yelled.

Joe didn't bother.

"Kill him! It's The Butcher!" a girl screamed.

The cop reacted—poorly to say the least—jerking his arms towards the sound and the girl's head exploded with a pop.

Another cop approached. A woman. "Joe?"

He paused. The voice was familiar. One he hadn't heard in a long, long time.

"Joe," the woman steeled up to the bonfire and the flames revealed her face. "It's me."

Dolly.

He looked at her through the sagging eyeholes of his mask. They'd had Chemistry together. She'd always made a point to be his partner for projects and labs, to talk to him. She'd been away that fateful night, some sort of Bible retreat or something her parents had forced her to attend.

Dolly. Dear Dolly. She was still wearing her cross.

"We have to take you in, Joe." She approached with handcuffs. Had she come here for him, to see him? After all this time.

He allowed her to cuff him, to put him into the back of the cop car. The other cop was crying.

"He's a monster!" A kid wailed. "He killed all of us! All of us!"

Joe rolled his eyes as the car pulled away. He wished he'd killed all of them. Then rest would be on the horizon. Instead, it was just the sun and another condemnation until the next Halloween.

As Dolly drove, Joe felt his body falling apart, turning to colourful leaves. He would return, of course. He always did.

Granny Mae, The Witch Bitch

My grandmother's house was a ramshackle affair, single storey, peeling paint, broken shutters, overgrown yard that probably drove her neighbours crazy. No wonder the neighbourhood kids called her a witch. And they didn't even know her.

'Cause I did and I knew she was worse.

My wrists still ached with phantom memory pains of her smacking them if I spoke too loudly, if I reached for an extra cookie (never freshly baked in that house), or if I left the chores too long. Yet my dad always made me visit, every other weekend, no matter how much I cried.

I took a key from my pocket, walking over the cracked front walk, and unlocked the door. I was still seething. Even after her death, Granny Mae was punishing me.

Her will demanded my subservience. I was the only granddaughter and "cleaning was a woman's job" stated her will, nothing would be paid out to the living relatives until the house was clean.

Dad was convinced Granny Mae was rich and so, here I was, on a bright autumn Saturday morning, to clean that bitch's house.

The door opened, revealing the living room.

It was just like I remembered, the last time I was there, over thirteen years ago. No TV, no couch (Granny Mae didn't like or even want visitors, besides me), just a buckling armchair, a stool (God, I hated that thing), and books. Books overflowing shelves, in waist high piles on the floor, and bottles. Bottles of wine and whiskey and scotch, all empty of alcohol—though some had been filled with sand and stones, bird bones and beads.

I sighed. This was going to take a while.

Beyond the living room was the kitchen, all the counter space taken up by empty boxes and more empty bottles. The dining room didn't have any furniture besides a folded cot—where I slept every weekend for years as a kid, surrounded by books. I continued on, feeling tired already just looking at all the shit I needed to box up or throw out.

A hall off the kitchen led to the back of the house, to the lone bedroom and bathroom. The bathroom was the single uncluttered room in the house, the white tiles were practically blindingly clean. The bedroom was as choked with books as the rest of the house, but had extras. Twigs had been tied together in strange configurations and hung on the walls, alongside dried herbs and flowers. Garlic bulbs hung on ropes in front of the window, like a weird hippie curtain. The bed was neatly made, as if waiting for Granny Mae to come back and find rest.

But she wouldn't be coming back and I couldn't find any piece of me to feel bad about it.

She'd been found a few blocks from here, three weeks ago in the early morning, stabbed. A mugging gone wrong—though, knowing Granny Mae, maybe it'd been one of the many people she'd pissed off.

I dropped the garbage bags I'd been carrying on the bed. May as well start here and get rid of her clothes first. I turned to the dresser and stopped.

The top of her dresser was clear and clean, besides for a single bottle of half finished whiskey. Cuthbert's Finest, 20 year. It sat, catching the light and casting amber hues across the wall. I smiled a bit.

Granny Mae would hate it if I had some, so I picked it up, uncorked it, and took a swig.

It was as I swallowed that I saw the salt circle on the dresser that had surrounded the bottle. I looked down at the bottle and saw that a strange symbol—like an ankh with an eye above it—had been scratched at the base of the neck.

The whiskey hit my belly, my nerves buzzed, and the hair on my arms rose. I could smell Granny Mae's deodorant, I felt a breath on the side of my neck, and then I fell.

Except I wasn't falling, I was sinking down in my own mind. My control, my self, my being shrunk and shrunk and shrunk until I was an observer in my own head, looking out my eyes, but detached.

In this way, I watched my hands put the bottle back on the dresser and sweep away the salt circle.

Granny Mae. I can't explain how I knew. But I knew. As if in a dream when knowledge is available to the dreamer and it is just true, in the same way I knew that Granny Mae had taken over.

She turned and took us to her closet, throwing open the door, and shoving aside the hanging shirts. Kneeling, she pressed a hand to a small section of the wall. Something clicked, then a corner of the wall swung open, revealing a deep compartment.

If I could gasp, or scream, or question, I would have. But I was a silent passenger in my own body as Granny Mae pulled out a sawed off shotgun, a box of shells, and three grenades.

Last, she pulled out a weathered leather journal.

Granny Mae stuffed the weapons into a black backpack, which she pulled on. The journal she carried to the bed and placed it on the neatly made covers. She tapped the cover twice.

Then we left, through the rooms and back out the front door, down the walk to the road.

Down the street, Granny Mae walked us both, taking us to her death site. I recognized it. Dad had driven me and my brothers by it and pointed it out.

"This is why you try and make nice with people, kids. So you don't end up like Granny Mae," he'd said.

Now, I never liked Granny Mae either, but even to me it'd sounded cold. She'd only been dead for a day at that point, her blood still a rusty stain on the sidewalk.

And today, the stain was just a ghost of a mark. Granny Mae didn't even look down at it as we walked over, going straight up the front walk to a massive McMansion, surrounded by carefully tended bushes and flowerbeds.

Without any hesitation, she knocked on the door. This can't be real, I thought. I'm dreaming. The whiskey was drugged. But I wasn't and it hadn't been. I knew this to be true.

The front door opened. A man stood in front of me and I recognized him. The mayor. His face was plastered everywhere, up for re-election.

"Can I help you?" he asked, looking me up and down, his hungry gaze making my skin crawl.

"Oh um, hi!" Granny Mae chirped, twirling a length of my hair around my index finger. "I'm doing, like, a school report and was hoping I could interview you?"

Is this how she thinks college students sound? Like valley girls? I was embarrassed for both of us. And terrified. Scared of what Granny Mae was planning, considering what she'd packed.

The mayor smiled—Johnny Borne was his name—and licked his lips. "Sure, honey. Why don't you come in?"

Granny Mae gave a little girl giggle and I became convinced that death had made her insane, that I was insane. We followed Mayor Borne inside his McMansion, the front room was all decadent marble and sculptures.

"So, what's your report about, honey?" Borne asked.

"Aren't you going to bring me somewhere more comfortable?" replied Granny Mae and if she wasn't already dead, I would have promised to murder her.

The Mayor grinned and led us deeper into the house, to a back office—walnut, leatherbound books, and plush chairs galore—gesturing us inside. Ceiling high windows looked out onto a perfectly manicured backyard and pool.

Granny Mae set her backpack down on a chair and leaned against it, cocking a hip. "Drink?"

Borne ate my body up in a glance and I wished I had the ability to vomit. What is with old dudes being so gross? Then he went over to a side table, where a decanter set sat. Granny Mae didn't waste any time. She'd always been someone to get straight to the point.

Pulling the shotgun out, she levelled it at Borne's back. He turned back, glasses in each hand, and froze.

"What the hell?" he snapped. "What the hell do you think you're doing?"

"Finishing what I started, Johnny," Granny Mae spat and for a brief moment my voice sounded exactly like hers.

Borne went pale. "No, it's impossible!"

"Let's not worry about what is and isn't impossible, kid." Granny Mae smirked. "Open the door."

"Go fuck yourself, Mae."

Granny Mae sighed. The same sigh she used every time before smacking my wrist, or yelling at me, and that's when I knew Johnny Borne would be regretting his words.

The shotgun went off, I'd never shot a gun before and I was shocked at its power, at the recoil. Borne went down, his left knee a crimson ruin. Granny Mae strode to him, grabbed his left wrist as he wailed, and dragged him over to a bookcase. Grabbing his collar, she yanked him up, and shoved him against the shelves, then she pressed the barrels of the gun against his neck.

Borne was crying, his chest hitching with tears. "Please don't kill me, Mae! I swear, it wasn't my idea! It was hers! I swear!"

"Open the door, kid, or I'll paint your fancy fake books with your blood."

The mayor nodded and reached for a crystal skull set between two copies of Dante's Inferno. He slipped the index and middle fingers of his right hand in either socket, which lit up, revealing fingerprint scanners. These scanned, beeped, flashed green. Granny Mae stepped back as the bookcase slid back and to the right, revealing a descending stone staircase.

"Please, Mae." The mayor had fallen to the floor without his support. "It was her, not me! Her!"

She looked down at him. Smiled. I felt bad for him then. Granny Mae's smiles were the worst. "Yeah, I know it, kid. You ain't smart enough. However, you did stab me and for that—" The next shotgun blast took his head, silencing his tears.

Down the stairs we went. Down and down and down. The air grew chilly, damp. Lights set in green-glass sconces guided us. Finally, at the bottom of the stairs was a small room that contained only a massive golden door.

Granny Mae reached into her bag and took out the grenades. My heart should have been racing with fear, I wanted to scream. Then she slowly, carefully, quietly, opened the door.

Inside was a huge sunken chamber, the middle of which contained a clear pool of green water that reflected the torchlight in golden flickers. Around its border were eggs, huge iridescent eggs waiting to hatch.

A woman stood in the middle of the pool, embracing a giant snake. The snake was massive, coiling around her limbs, and rather than a snake's visage, it had a somewhat human-like face, albeit deformed and grotesque. Fangs stuck out from its lips and its eyes glittered black in the flickering light, showing a malevolent intelligence.

"Hey hun, am I interrupting something?" Granny Mae used the same tone she'd used on me when she'd catch me on my phone, rather than cleaning.

The woman turned, arms still wrapped around her lover. "Who — oh." She smirked. "Mae. Didn't expect to see you back here."

Behind my back, Granny Mae's grip tightened on the grenades. "I'll be fair, Lisbeth. When I came here last, I never expected this and, for sure, it caught me by surprise. You play the helpless victim quite well."

Lisbeth shrugged, snapped her fingers. The eggs around the pool began to shiver, the life inside of them roiled, readying to wake. "Let's be real, Mae, you are—were old. Old-fashioned. So you assumed my husband was to blame. You deserved what you got."

I mean she isn't wrong about you, Granny.

Granny Mae sighed. Whether at the woman's statement or mine, I didn't know.

"Either way, I can't leave you and your spawn here to eat up the town. I do still have family," she replied.

"Cute. Protecting a family that hates you." Lisbeth stroked the flank of her lover, who hissed. "Whose body is that anyways? I'd hate to kill her without knowing her name."

"Grenade," replied Granny Mae.

"What?" Lisbeth frowned.

The grenades bounced along the stone floor, one came to rest near a shivering egg, two skittered to the corners of the rooms, and she let one drop right by my feet. Granny Mae didn't wait, turning and sprinting up the stairs. My heart thundered in my chest, my lungs heaved as we raced towards the exit.

The woman screamed, her hate and anger chasing us. Granny Mae glanced back once, just as the grenades exploded, shaking the whole building. The snake man was just behind us, his face snarled up with rage, his fangs bared and dripping poison. Then a block of concrete fell from the ceiling, crushing him to the stairs. The staircase crumbled, one or two of the grenades must have destroyed some vital support section or beam, because now Granny Mae was racing against the destruction.

Despite how much my body ached, how my lungs burned, she never stopped. She fought through the pain and stress, throwing us through the open door way as the stairs completely gave way and the passage was filled with debris.

Even then, she didn't stop. She carried us out onto the backyard, over the fence, through the back streets, and back to her home. Only then, inside and safe from witnesses, did she allow my body to collapse to the floor.

We rested there for a while, then she pushed us up again. Took us back to her bedroom.

"Damn but it feels good to be young again," she said to herself, or me, I don't know.

She picked up the bottle of Cuthbert's Finest. "One more for the road."

And with a gulp, she was gone, and I fell back into myself, into my aching body, my burning lungs, and I fell to the floor, dropping the whiskey. Crying.

It took a week to get Granny Mae's house in order. I let the relatives pick over and take what they wanted (which wasn't anything, I'm pretty sure they were just hoping to find jewelry or treasures), but I kept the journal secret. The journal Granny Mae had placed on her bed and tapped, to make sure I'd look at it.

A journal that outlined who she had been, what she had done, and all the things she'd killed that went bump in the night.

Oh and it turned out she did have a shit ton of money. And it all went to me.

I can't say I grew to love Granny Mae. She was still a bitch.

But I guess I could understand her just a little.

And with what she showed me in her journal, I learned to be a lot more wary of the shadows of the world.

State of Alarm

GARTEK WILL NOW COMMENCE ITS ANNUAL PERSONAL ALARM SYSTEM TEST.

BE ADVISED. THIS IS ONLY A TEST.

Across the nation, half the population slowed and stopped what it was doing. It was 2:30p.m. on a warm summer afternoon. In each city, in each town, things were calm and quiet. After the murder cult killed two hundred people three years ago, a large percentage of the population had elected to have Gartek's innovative personal alarm and GPS tracker installed in their sternums. Gartek guaranteed action within five minutes should the user say their pre-decided panic word and did not answer their phone immediately after.

GARTEK WILL NOW TEST ALL ACTIVE IMPLANTS IN

...3...

The murder cult tried to continue operations, but Gartek responded within minutes and were able to track down kidnappers before they could cut the implant out of their victims. Then the Gartek specialists would deal with the cultists with utmost aggression while police looked the other way. It only took a few months for the cult to all but disappear and so, more people got the implant.

...2...

Every year, Gartek initiated a test for users to let them know if their implant required replacement. It was seen by the users as a minor inconvenience, like renewing a license or paying a bill. All it took was a single Gartek employee to check that the frequency was correct and press a button.

This year, Dennis Waterman had been assigned this job. He was hungover from the wild night he'd had before and stumbled into the office late and with a pounding head. Dennis sat down at the small metal counter in the tiny concrete room and looked at the screen that zipped through graphs, profiles, and metrics. It was all a foreign language to him. On the counter in front of him was the frequency dial and a large red button upon which read "TEST".

He squinted at the screen and tried to focus on the frequency readout. His head spun. He read a 9 as a 6 and adjusted the dial as he thought was necessary and, with a sigh, pressed the button.

...1...

The test started as normal. From the chests of millions of people came a blaring siren, almost exactly like that the city used for tornado drills, but at a safe audible level. At first, the users smiled as they glanced down. All was well, their tech was working, they were safe. The test continued past the normal thirty seconds.

The siren began to grow louder, rising in a shrill shriek. Across the nation, the cacophony overwhelmed everyone, reaching even the ears of the passengers on planes that flew overhead, echoing upward and ever higher, before dissipating into the cosmos.

Those without the transplants clutched at their ears, trying to protect themselves against the pain of the aural assault. Those with it clutched their chests as their sternums shattered against the powerful vibrations. Their hearts thundered in rebellion against the violation, but inevitably failed.

One by one they fell, some flat on their faces, shattering nose cartilage like fine china on pavement, and some onto their backs, their skulls thudding in a way that should have been audible but wasn't over the hellish noise.

It took Dennis only three minutes and six seconds to figure out where the override emergency cut-off switch was: under the metal counter and at the right-hand back corner. The majority of Gartek clientele were dead within two minutes and forty-seven seconds. Any survivors died soon after from heart failure.

Those without the implant, but within critical range of a victim, were deaf for the rest of their lives. Those just outside the critical range suffered a range of symptoms; tinnitus, reduced hearing, crippling migraines, and nosebleeds.

The next year, Gartek went bankrupt instead of paying out the lawsuit filed against them by the victims' families. A new company emerged six months after that, offering high-end, state-of-the-art hearing aids. They were called AudioTek.

Suffer No Harm

The Stranger was dusty with the roads he'd travelled, his face grimed with weeks between baths. The bartender of the Loose Skirts Saloon—a thin man named Cecil with a carefully trimmed mustache—watched him lay hands on Sweet Peach, now the youngest lady working, with a flinch. Lady Red, who sat at the honky-tonk piano, dancing out a tune, watched the Stranger as well, her smile easy, gentle, perfect. A graveyard chill ran over Cecil and he tasted sour copper at the back of his tongue. Clearing his throat, Cecil pulled a bottle of whiskey from a shelf. His hands shook, a leaf in strong winds predicting a storm.

The Stranger yanked Sweet Peach between the tables in a rough mockery of a dance, hands clutching at her hip and back. She tried to push away, laughed when she couldn't, as if it were all good fun. But her laugh rang false.

The other five ladies were engaged in their own activities: Tammy Lee dealt cards for Old 'Baccy Joe and his friends, Jester Ann regaled a full table of cattle drivers with raucous tales, and raven-haired Betsy Bee was at the bar matching Dr. Ambridge shot for shot. Up on the second floor, Juliet and Clementine were plying their trade.

But despite being busy, Cecil knew the women on the first floor were watching the Stranger. Watching him pull Sweet Peach around. Taking his measure.

Cecil tapped two glasses down on the scarred counter and uncorked the whiskey.

"Stranger," he called and the man glanced across the tables at him. "Wet yer whistle with me."

The Stranger stopped and Sweet Peach pulled out of his arms, slipping through the tables like a snake, to sit by Lady Red's side. The other woman wrapped an arm around Sweet Peach, playing with one hand. In Lady Red's protection, without breaking her smile, Sweet Peach began to sing along to the piano. The Stranger frowned, watching his quarry escape, then sauntered to the bar, taking no care and knocking into several occupied chairs.

Cecil poured two glasses of the amber liquid, slid one in front of the Stranger. He didn't bother to smile.

"Thanks, boy," the Stranger said and knocked back the alcohol.

Cecil poured him another.

"How much—" the Stranger interrupted himself with a rancid burp. "How much for that whore?"

Nodding at Sweet Peach, the Stranger held out his glass, and Cecil obliged with more whiskey.

"The women set their own prices and manage their own business." Cecil hadn't touched his own drink. He only watched the Stranger suck up the free alcohol like a horse to water after a long, hard run. "Round Bitterbend, you'd best be careful of crossing the wrong path."

"Whose path? That whore's?" The Stranger barked out a harsh laugh and pulled back his stained duster. Underneath: a small pistol in bad need of a clean and oil, jammed in a dirty holster.

"You wonder why Bitterbend has no Sheriff? Sit a spell." Cecil refilled the Stranger's glass again. Better the bastard be drunk than dead by the end of the night. "I'll tell you."

ON THE FIRST DAY

A blight came to Bitterbend. When the Sheriff arrived, it drizzled some, not enough to be helpful, just enough to be uncomfortable. Jonah Jebediah had the face of a vulture, all sharp angles, a long hooked nose, and cruel black eyes. A hungry look about him. Always.

He came here, to the saloon, after getting settled. He came straight to where you're standing now, Stranger, and he grabbed me by my collar and yanked me near clear over the counter.

"Listen here, boy." I could smell the 'baccy chew on his breath. "Only ways I'll tolerate whores in *my* town is if I get to make sure the product is worth the real estate. Do you get my meaning?"

"I'm not the owner of this saloon, sir," I told him and he let go of my collar.

I caught myself from falling. I'll tell you, Stranger, that my heart was racing faster than ever I've known.

"Get the owner then, boy," Jebediah said and spat brown 'baccy juice onto my freshly cleaned floor. "Don't waste my time now."

"The owner isn't in town."

His fist struck, lightning made flesh. I hit the floor, my jaw throbbing, blood on my tongue and a tooth loose. That's the type of man Jonah Jebediah had been.

The Sheriff came back that same night. I'd already warned the ladies. Back then there were eight of them.

Lady Red stood when Jebediah entered. He was followed by six others, men we knew, that we'd known. He'd made short work of finding allies in Bitterbend but then, a rat always multiplies and the West is full of yellow-bellies looking for someone to follow. I won't bother with their names. They're as dead as Jebediah, dust to the wind and all that.

But they came in here as bold as brass, seven men ready for a fight, and Lady Red didn't even flinch.

"What a pretty bunch of whores," Jebediah said, getting right into her face. "But you're a bit old for my tastes."

He spat 'baccy right onto the hem of Lady Red's dress. His rats snickered. Red, though, she's got nerves of steel, didn't even flinch. I think the Sheriff was unnerved by that. Most likely angered too. A man like Jebediah wasn't used to people standing up to him. He was used to them falling in line.

The Sheriff walked around her and looked at the other ladies, they stood just up there, along the railing on the second floor hallway. Jebediah pointed at Honey, she was the youngest of them, barely eighteen and only six months in town.

"I'll take that one," Jebediah said and the hungry look on his face grew.

Poor Honey went pale and stepped back, hiding behind Jester Ann.

"You'll not be taking anyone, Sheriff," Red said. "I don't like the look of you so I think we shall refuse your patronage."

The Sheriff's face snarled up and he bared tombstone teeth stained yellow. "The fuck you talking about, girl?"

"You can leave now. We're closed tonight." Lady Red stared down the rats at the door and I can tell you, Stranger, her stare is not something to dismiss.

In the moment that followed, time crawled. I heard the building creak in the dry wind that growled down from the north and the squeak of the Sheriff's teeth as he clenched them tight. Then he smiled. He tipped his hat.

"We'll be back," he promised and led the way through the saloon's double swinging doors into the night.

"There'll be trouble, Lady Red," I told her.

Red looked up to the second floor, at the other ladies.

"We can handle it." But I seen how her hands were clenched, how pale her face was.

Lady Red—a veteran at the Loose Skirts saloon, used to dealing with drunks, vagabonds, outlaws, and worse—was worried. And that scared me more than the Sheriff's smile.

ON THE SECOND DAY

That trouble came the next night. You see, Honey had a sweetheart. The pastor's son no less. They thought they were so sneaky, meeting at night, in the church. But we all knew. The pastor was pressuring his son to save the young girl, get married, start a family and rescue her from sin.

The Sheriff got her while she was on her way back home. One of the rats surely told him.

I won't go into the details, Stranger. It'd be enough to make any man's stomach turn. I'll say this for Honey, she fought him. She was a good girl, a brave girl. She fought. He beat her bloody, broke her sweet face, and strangled her. Honey ended up dead, but the Sheriff wound up with a face clawed to ribbons and none of the prize he was looking for.

That made him mad. It must have.

ON THE THIRD DAY

That's when we found her. He had strung Honey up right out there from the porch roof, so's we'd find her in the morning, naked, cold, dead. Her blood painted the planks, her tears dewed her cheeks, deep bruises calicoed her skin. The women didn't allow anyone to touch Honey. They cut her down and locked up the saloon. Bitterbend was tense. It was a stand-off, you see. The Sheriff made it clear. Give him what he wants or be strung up like poor Honey who'd told him no.

I stayed here, behind the bar all day, with my dead pa's shotgun. Chances were I'd blow my own foot off before getting the Sheriff, but I had to try. The women of Loose Skirts have always been good to the Lockner family, y'see.

No one came by. Not the Sheriff, not any regulars, not the pastor.

At dusk, Lady Red sent me home. The air was heavy. The horizon was black with churning clouds and the distant thunder that rolled through the ground. Something was coming. I could see it in the look on Lady Red's face. Taste it in the lightning on the air. Hear it in the silence of Bitterbend.

My house, well, it's just behind the saloon. The Lockners have lived there for generations. We've been the caretakers for the Loose Skirts saloon for as long as I can remember. That's not important to the story, what's important is that my front door looks over the back lot where Tammy Lee grows the vegetables for the saloon.

It was the sound that woke me.

Through the thunder and the crash of rain on the roof, through the growling storm, I heard the whispering. Like snakes hissing. Hundreds, thousands of snakes.

It was late and dark as anything. But I was awake. See this hair on my arms? It had risen like Christ himself on that third day. At first, I fumbled for the candle, but as I found my box of matches, I couldn't bring myself to break the darkness. It all felt different, y'see. Not natural. And to shatter that with light? Blasphemy of the highest order.

I stumbled down the hall to the front door. The whispers went deep and low, they made the very floorboards shiver and my heart skipped a beat. Opening the door, rain hit my face like icy buckshot.

They were out there, in the storm.

The Loose Skirts women knelt in a circle, as naked as when they were born. Overhead, purple lightning laced through clouds, throbbing like a living thing as thunder roared. Their hair flowed loose over their backs, rain crashed over their bodies and, I'll promise you this on my mother's grave, their skin glowed like moonlight. They were as stars in the storm-darkened night.

Right hands raised, the seven women swayed, twisting their bodies like snakes dancing to a flute. I could see knives in their hands, strange things, as thin as splinters and the purest silver. I could hear the beat in my head. It strummed through me, hm-hm-HMM. Something like that.

Their other hands pinned large, brilliantly coloured snakes to the mud. The animals writhed and snapped, their fangs as bright as the blades that hovered above them.

Down the knives slashed, slicing the serpents in two, from jaw to tip of tail. The women scooped out tiny organs and tossed them to the middle of the circle, then stuffed vibrant purple flowers into the serpents.

Hands stained crimson rose, fingertips straining for the boiling clouds above. The chanting grew louder, a heartbeat tempo for the heart of the storm, their bodies swayed, dropped, slithered in the mud, limbs entwining as their voices ascended and called and called. My racing heart became the bass, thump-thump thump-thump, and they twisted around the dead snakes, blood in mud in hair on faces, ululating. And somewhere in the distance, even through the thunder, I heard something answer.

I ain't ashamed to admit that I fled, hid beneath my blankets as a child might.

ON THE FOURTH DAY

Jebediah and his men came in the morning. They found the doors locked so they broke those two front windows. See this scar above my eye? One of the bricks they threw struck me there, knocked me near senseless.

He sent some of his men around back and they tore up Tammy

Lee's garden and broke my windows too.

The Sheriff didn't come in though. His goal wasn't to break in. It was to terrorize.

ON THE FIFTH DAY

With midday came Rattlesnake Renee on a horse as black as night. She wore a jacket and pants of snakeskin, a necklace of fangs round her neck, a wide brim hat to ward off the sun. Her left cheek was scarred where she'd been bit and poisoned by a rattler. Yet survived. I see the recognition in your eyes, Stranger. Yes, she is one and the same.

The Rattlesnake Renee. Bounty hunter and, as it happens, the owner of the Loose Skirts Saloon. A woman of towering stature and flaxen hair, skin kissed harshly by the sun.

High noon, she rode into Bitterbend and met Sheriff Jebediah right in front of the saloon. I was here, I watched it all.

"Who the hell are you?" he asked.

Renee swung over, hit the road, sent up puffs of dust, no sign of the rain that had come the night before.

She kept one hand on her saddle. Her eyes, green as poison, watched Jebediah like prey. She said nothing.

"I don't 'ppreciate strangers in my town, y'hear, girl?" he continued.

Behind him gathered his six cowardly men, as predictable as shit follows a pig. Renee's jacket caught the sunlight on its scales, glittering like gemstones, and she said nothing, just stayed as still as a snake in grass.

"You deaf, whore?" He took one step, a second step.

Renee's hand—the one that had rested on her saddle—slashed forward. In it, a whip made of snake skin.

It lashed Jebediah's face, cut it open like a knife through butter, and his skin curdled away from a scarlet wound, blood rained down to the ground in crimson drops.

He screamed like a child, clutching his head, stumbled back.

It took a second, Stranger. I watched it from that window right there.

The Sheriff howled like a mad beast and looked up at Renee through stained hands. His posse fell on him, pulled him away, down the road in the direction of Doc Ambridge's place by the general store.

I knew he'd be back. And with more hate than ever.

Renee tied off her horse in front of the saloon, pulling her bags from the saddle.

"Cecil," she said as she entered, boots hammering on the floor. "Keep an eye on my horse. Keep the saloon locked. We're not to be disturbed."

I stayed up that night, shotgun in hand, behind this very bar. Jebediah didn't come that night. I reckon the stitches and sedatives the doc gave him kept him down.

I wish I could say it was a quiet night. They sang. For hours. It wasn't English, wasn't any kind of language I could understand.

And they danced, at least, I have to assume that's what the sound was. The sound of flesh sliding around and around on floorboards. Because if it wasn't their bare feet then...well.

ON THE SIXTH DAY

Rattlesnake Renee left. She'd spent the night. Slipped out silently as I slept on the floor behind the bar. A five-dollar bill was left on the counter. Renee always left me gifts when she visited, as a child it'd been candy, now it was cash. Not that I'm complaining.

Lady Red came down when I began to sweep. She put seven glasses on the bar.

"Cecil." She turned to me and grabbed my hands, her eyes caught me like a fly in a web. "See these glasses and heed me. We are opening tonight and when Jebediah and his men come—and they will—you will serve them at no cost. But you will serve them with these glasses and none other. Understand?"

The glasses were delicate, pretty things with nary a crack or chip. Each caught the light streaming through the window and glistened with faint oily colours.

"Allow no other to drink from them, Cecil."

Returning upstairs, Red left me with the glasses. I picked them up, one by one, and placed them on a shelf behind the bar. As I did, I saw that each had a tiny drawing etched on the bottom: a snake biting its own tail, forming a circle. Each smelled faintly of something acidic.

Sheriff Jebediah arrived at dusk with his minions in tow. I was behind the bar. The regulars were at their tables and the ladies were their usual selves. Lady Red stood from the piano and came to the bar when she saw them enter. She braced a foot against a stool, allowing her dress to shift and show skin. Calculated, you see. As calculated as a snake's rattle.

The sheriff was in a state. Renee's snakeskin whip left a diagonal slash through his face, which Doc Ambridge had tried his best to stitch up. Jebediah's skin was blotchy, angry, and the right corner of his mouth was caught up in a sneer from the injury. It suited him, that sneer. It suited just fine.

"Welcome Sheriff," Lady Red said, as sweet as sugar. "Cecil, pour the Sheriff and his men some whiskey. Top shelf and on the house, of course."

Think what you may, Stranger, but I did it. I took those seven glasses down and filled them each with my best whiskey. I didn't care what happened to Jebediah but I felt a pang for those spineless men who'd chosen to fall in line with him. I'd grown up with some of them. Been to a couple of their weddings.

"I think we got off on the wrong foot, Sheriff." Lady Red gestured at the glasses I'd laid out. "I'm of a mind to rectify that mistake."

Time stopped. A hiccup in the world. Jebediah's eyes narrowed. Then the other ladies stood and went to the men behind the Sheriff, pressing against them, smiling. The Sheriff's eyes crawled up Lady Red's thigh. He licked his lips and the bottom of his cut leaked blood onto his tongue. He smiled.

"Damn right." Jebediah spat on the floor and strode to the bar, finishing his drink in one gulp. "Look what that bitch did to me!"

I refilled his glass, just as I've been with yours, Stranger.

"I'm sure I can make it up to you, Sheriff," she replied. "In fact, I can guarantee it."

His men joined him at my bar, drinking from their glasses. Their eyes roamed over the ladies' bodies, hungry and oblivious. Every time a glass was emptied, I filled it.

The sheriff's hand whipped out and he grabbed the back of Lady Red's head, dragging her close. A thread of blood ran from his wound, over his lips, and dripped from his chin. Whatever he saw in her eyes, he let go in a hurry, but kept his smile and threw back the third glass I poured him.

"Let's go then, whore."

Seven glasses on the bar, empty. Seven men and women disappearing upstairs.

I closed up early that night and sent my regulars home. I locked up. I went to my house and sat against the front door and watched the shadows move behind the curtains on the second floor until I slept an uneasy sleep plagued by the hissing of snakes.

ON THE SEVENTH DAY

The sun rose. I woke up and went to the saloon. There were seven bodies hung from the front of the jail. All seven men were naked, slit from jaw to pelvis. Their bloated faces were contorted in chilling expressions of agony, their eyes were stained red with burst vessels, and their tongues—Lord—their tongues were swollen so large that they stuck out from between each man's lips. And if you looked closely, Stranger, you could see an oiliness to their tongues and a sheen of strange colours.

And that's not all. Their organs were set in delicate piles directly below their heads, a purple flower placed on top of each. Each man had a snake jammed into his slit throat, the serpentine tail hanging down like a bizarre tongue.

Three wives and three mothers wept for their husbands and sons but said nothing. Four children wailed for their dead fathers. But the people of Bitterbend accepted the fallout of the standoff that had gone on for those seven days. We buried our foolish six in our graveyard and burned the Sheriff in the street.

Now look up, Stranger, see those glasses and mind that, in Bitterbend, no harm may come to the ladies of the Loose Skirts saloon.

Cecil finally picked up his own glass and tossed back the whiskey. Lady Red moved on to a rag-time song and Sweet Peach got up to dance. But the Stranger didn't move. He stared at the row of seven glasses, set between two bottles of the saloon's finest whiskey, three shelves up.

"So, if you're interested, I am sure the ladies would be happy to accommodate, Stranger," Cecil said. "As long as you're respectful."

The Stranger gulped down the last of his whiskey and slapped a five-dollar bill on the bar.

"It's late," the Stranger replied, quietly. "I mean to hit the road at dawn so..."

With that, Cecil watched the Stranger stumble out of the saloon. Betsy Bee waved Cecil down to where she sat next to Dr. Armitage, who was passed out on the bartop. Betsy held out her shot glass, which

Cecil faithfully refilled.

"You scared away a customer, Cece!" she said with a theatrical pout. "You should work on your conversation skills."

Cecil just smiled and refilled her glass once more.

Hide and Seek

I had to pee again. I knew it wasn't a real need. It was how scared I was. I peered down another silent street. The lights were off in every house, even though my dino watch said it was only 6pm.

I shivered.

It was dark. The streetlights flickered, dimmed.

I went up to a house that still had jack-o-lanterns with flickering candles. I rang the doorbell and heard it chime. I knocked and no one came.

Pressed my knees together, I didn't need to pee. But it felt like it.

I turned and left.

Stripped trees creaked in rising winds that sent showers of damp leaves over the sidewalks.

There should have been other kids. Grown ups.

My pillowcase barely had any candy in it, but it still felt so heavy.

I was lost. Every street was dark. We'd only just moved here a week ago.

After Joan's funeral.

My parents said we needed a fresh start. I just knew I hated Joan even more dead than when she'd been alive.

She'd always been their favourite.

I sat on a curb and pulled some candy out of my bag, checking it like Mom taught me, so I wouldn't eat a razor blade. I tried to remind my body, I didn't actually need to pee.

In fact, thinking I did was what got me into this mess.

I didn't really want to go trick or treating tonight. I didn't have any friends. I didn't want to go alone. But going alone in my old Batman costume was better than staying home and listening to Mom cry.

I always felt like peeing when I was scared. It started with Joan's favourite game: hide and seek. I always had to be the one hiding. She said it was because I was younger. But if she caught me, she would pin me down and pinch me with pliers until I screamed.

So I hid and shook, and hoped she wouldn't find me and that Dad would come home soon.

By the fifth house, being asked again where my friends were, I really thought I needed to pee. So when my math teacher, Ms. Smalls, opened the next door, I asked to use her bathroom.

I didn't pee. I just cried.

Then I flushed and pretended to wash my hands. When I came out, everyone was gone.

I swallowed the candy and realized how thirsty I am. The candy only made it worse.

Somewhere down the street, someone giggled.

I stood, listening, heart pounding.

The giggle repeated.

I turned from the sound and ran.

My watch said 8pm. I really had to pee and the giggles were getting closer. I turned down another dark street, my candy bag abandoned a long time ago. I didn't bother knocking at any more doors. No one was answering.

She was catching up.

Snot poured down my lips and chin. I turned down a side yard and spotted a small wooden hutch pressed against the side of the house.

I couldn't see what time it was. I squirmed in the rotting vegetables and coffee grounds, trying to filter the smell through my costume.

I couldn't hear anything, maybe she'd gone away.

Then the lid was pulled away.

I was yanked out by my hair and she stood over me in the same dress Mom picked out for her to be buried in.

"Found you!" she said, pliers in hand.

As she gripped my throat and lowered the pliers to my face, hot liquid gushed over my thighs, soaking my costume.

Only Way

Our greed took the light from us and plunged our world into an endless night of ash and cold.

Wrapped in what rags I could find, I pushed against the wind, through trees as sharp as blades. Even through my clothes, I could taste the sour ash—sins of generations past that still cursed us.

Behind me, our leaning house was swallowed in the forever night. He was back there, lungs rotting from darkcough. It could be weeks, or days, but he would die if I didn't find tinea weed in time. If I could even find it at all.

Through the dark wood, whose branches creaked and cracked like ancient bones. A lank quadruped followed, slinking through the ash and weed. It could have been a mutated wolf or even a deer. It didn't matter. In this new world, we were all slaves to the night.

When I grew tired, thighs aching from dragging my legs through the deep ash, I climbed a tree and tied myself to its ragged trunk. Pulling my arms in through my sleeves, I huddled into my jacket and rags. I could smell myself, but my musk was better than the acrid air around me.

Somewhere below me, something growled.

I plucked some dried meat from an inner pocket and slipped it between my lips, chewing slowly. Favouring my right jaw, where the teeth wiggled and gums bled more freely. Eventually I fell asleep, meat half chewed in my cheek.

LEGENDS SAY IT CAN BE found deep in the wood, near where our greedy ancestors had sliced into the valleys and bedrock. That's where I went.

Though I wasn't sure if I was striving to find it or just to stay away from home so I wouldn't have to watch him slowly die.

I didn't know if I was a saviour or a coward.

The beast had circled my tree while I slept. I saw its circuit in the ash. I shimmied down and began my march again.

On this lonely journey, I couldn't keep my thoughts blank. One ear and eye open for the predator that followed behind, my mind whirled. It chased a familiar circuit, the same one since I was a child.

Resentment to my parents, who had children despite everything. I didn't ask to be born into this world, to be born to suffer, to despair. He's the same way. He wants to have kids. Even now, spitting up bits of lung, he brought it up before I left. Begged me not to go, to think of the future. If he dies, I'd be bringing up the child alone. It didn't matter to him. He didn't even consider how hard it would be for me. All that mattered was the idea that a part of him would be carried forward.

I left anyway. If I had to suffer in this world, I would try my best to keep him here too.

THE LAND SLOPED DOWNWARD. THAT'S when it attacked. When it had the high ground.

I heard it growl. I turned, too late, and it was on me, slobbering jaws snapping at my throat. I gripped its fur with two white knuckled fists, holding it just barely at bay.

Dozens of milk-white eyes swirled in sunken sockets, blind, it had to have tracked me by sound and smell alone. Didn't matter.

My third arm, the one that sat in the middle of sternum, darted out from my jacket. It held the knife I always kept ready. I buried the blade deep into its throat.

It howled, trying to pull away. I let its momentum roll us over, until I was on top. Pinning it down.

I sliced it chin to groin, let its organs spill steaming to be coated by the acidic ash.

I stood, straddling it, reaching into its body. I harvested the organs that seemed the least riddled with boils and worms, slipping the meat into my oiled pouches, tying them tight until I could cook them later.

I left the rest for whatever else was starving in these woods.

I found myself in a valley, where a river used to be. Back when rivers were above ground. Here, the land was partially protected by hills and thicker trees so that the ash was less.

A relic of the past hung over the dusty riverbed like a skeletal cowl. A shattered bridge, its metal beams curled and rusting. I took shelter beneath it, away from any eyes that could be watching.

I cleared an area, made a pile from some petrified wood, and started myself a fire to cook the meat I'd been so lucky to get.

I sensed it before I saw it. The hair on the back of my three arms rose. I looked up.

It perched on the bridge above me, towering. Blacker than the dark sky. And in the blackest abyss, glowed two crimson eyes. Massive antennae rose over a body not much more human than mine, covered in a dark thick fur.

My mouth instantly dried up, I scooted back, jagged metal digging into my spine. I knew I couldn't hide from it. It saw beyond the physical. It saw beyond all. I could feel it in the deepest part of my brain.

It spread its wings, blotting out more sky, and it descended gracefully, landing delicately on two taloned feet. It stood across my fire from me. I gripped my knife with a sweaty hand knowing it would do me no good.

Tucking its wings back against its body, it stared.

Its stare trapped me. Then the pressure shifted and I realized it wasn't looking at me anymore. It was staring at the fire.

Slowly, painfully slow, I reached forward and pulled a hunk of meat from a steaming stone, singing my fingers. I tossed it.

The giant caught it with three fingered paws. It turned from me, launching itself to perch on a nearby stone. Hunched over the meat. Eating.

I stood, as slowly as I had reached for the meat. I crept forward. Its generous haunches were covered in the dark fur that caught the firelight so softly. I reached out and pinched a bit in my fingers, pulling until the prize came free.

What I now held was a hybrid of feather and fur, covered in a fine coating of dust or ash. I slipped it between my lips, unable to help myself. I chewed, swallowed. I don't know what I expected.

Stepping back, away from it, I probed my body, tongued my teeth.

My gums were firm. The taste of copper only an afterthought.

My teeth weren't loose.

My joints felt refreshed.

This was it. The cure.

I then knew. Tinea weed wasn't a plant at all.

It was a monster.

The chewing stopped and it turned, eyes blazing over a shoulder.

I tossed it another hunk of meat.

I could grab more fur. I could make the long trek home. I could cure him, submit to him, bear his children.

Or I could follow this dark harbinger. I could hunt for it. It could keep me well in this wasteland for as long as it found me useful, its crimson eyes a beacon in the night.

The choice wasn't really a choice.

I threw it the last bit of meat I had.

I wasn't going back. Ever again. The only way I would go was forward.

Left Behind

The tires of my sedan hum on the road as it ribbons onward into the heavy night. Riverdale Road is sparse in the way of streetlights and fellow travellers. It's a lonely stretch. A few houses have been built on the west side, while shadowed fields on the east gave credit to the eerie legends I'd read about it. Roads like these are the bread and butter of America's ghostly roadmap. I smile a bit to myself. I should make sure to remember that and add it to my scrapbook. I glance over at my boyfriend, Alan, who is entranced at whatever it is that he has pulled up on his phone. He's not the ghostchaser type but he loves me enough to come along on my adventures.

"You can pull up anywhere around here, Claire," Zora says from the backseat.

"What about the gates?"

Zora's boyfriend, Ross, chuckles a bit, causing the familiar, bright flicker of anxiety to nip at me.

"Did I say something wrong?"

"Well, the "Gates of Hell" don't actually exist anymore. This place has pretty much all changed since that guy killed his wife. I mean, there was no reason to keep them up after the guy burned his own house to the ground. The gates were just these little rusty things from what I hear, nothing to write home about," Zora says. "Really, it seems like supernatural activity happens anywhere along the length of the road so this should be good enough. Look, there's a mile marker right there. Maybe we'll see one of those bloody handprints that are supposed to appear on all the road signs."

To my left, distant house lights twinkle, a vague reminder of civilization. I activate my turning signal despite there being no one else on the road and pull onto the dirt. I turn off the car and the four of us sit there in the shadowed interior of my sedan. I feel a momentary flutter in my belly, wishing I'd come here with only Alan. We'd just moved here for Alan's work. I was working odd jobs and, otherwise, being introverted. Alan keeps saying that we needed to get out more, make friends, so here I was... trying to make friends.

I take a deep breath and open my door. After a moment, the other three passengers do the same. The four of us step out into the night. Summer's warm touch is still present in the small breeze that sends the field grass whispering. Alan yawns and stretches out his arms.

"Want me to grab the bag?" he asks and starts to the back of the car without waiting for my answer.

I take a second to gaze out at the field where, supposedly, a man went mad and murdered his wife and children. The familiar thrill of fear rolls down my body and I savour it. Getting the creeps from a ghost story was preferable to the daily anxieties I feel in my life.

"Everyone got their flashlight?" Ross asks.

I don't know either of them very well and that puts me on edge. Alan met Zora through work and had mentioned to her that I loved urban legends and haunted houses. She had told him about the cursed stretch of road near Thornton called Riverdale. Next thing I knew, we were going on double dates. Zora was alright, carefree if a bit arrogant, but Ross was not the type of guy I usually make friends with. Still, Alan wanted me to try. Try and make friends.

"Well, let's go and bust some ghosts." Alan pulls out the little backpack I'd brought and tosses me the camera before shutting the trunk.

The plastic equipment smarts as it hits my hands. It's my clunky polaroid camera that I'd gotten at a second-hand shop. One of my favourite things to do is try and capture things on film. People will always claim it's fake if it's digital so I only ever take polaroids. Plus, it makes for good scrapbook material.

I can't help but smile and Alan gives me a wink. I toss him the car keys, which he catches easily.

"Keep that in the backpack, okay? I wouldn't want to lose it and have us trapped out here for the ghosties!" I laugh.

I lead the way off the dirt of the breakdown lane and into the thick grass. To keep my hands free, I have a headlamp on.

"Zora, you said you've been here before, right?" I say, feeling responsible to make sure everyone is having fun and feeling entertained, because this is my hobby and they are only here because I asked them to come.

"Yeah, but I didn't see anything. Not a single devious jogger, bloody-handed boy, or lady in white either. Really, Claire, I don't know why you find all this dumb shit so fun," she says with a small laugh.

"I heard that the lady everyone sees at the side of the road is the ghost of the man's wife, looking for her children, or maybe her husband for revenge!" Ross says, punctuating the last word with a theatrical cackle.

"I feel like if the city bothered to add more streetlights along the road then no one would be "seeing" these ghoulies anymore," Alan says. "People watch too many horror movies."

"We should have come on a full moon, then maybe we could have seen a werewolf too," Ross chimes in.

I tell myself it doesn't matter that they think I'm silly for wanting to believe in this kind of stuff. Ahead of me, the field stretches on and disappears into a dark void. The moon is covered in thick clouds so that the only true light is from the flashlights, which sweep in savage beams over the grass and weeds. I have walked farther ahead from the others, trying to find that same delicious shiver, that same sense of foreboding that I had before, but the others are laughing and talking too loudly. Any sense of atmosphere has been smashed to bits.

"You know, maybe we will see that old madman after all. From the version I heard, his wife was blonde. Maybe he'll think you're his wife come home and come out for a nice, big kiss!" Zora jumps at me, hands curled up in claws.

I scream and hate myself for falling for such a childish trick. "That's not funny, okay?"

"No, honestly! Look!" Zora is laughing as she shoves her phone towards my face.

Curiosity was always my greatest weakness, just call me Pandora, so I take the phone. She has a browser open to some ghost story site. The header of this particular post reads "FAMILY HAUNTS RIVERDALE ROAD." Underneath that is an image, which seems to be a poor photocopy of an actual hardcopy photo. In it, a family is standing in a line a few feet in front of a partially completed house. The solemn stiff-backed father, supposedly the one who went insane, is on the right. Next to him are two bored looking children holding hands. On the very left is the mother, a kind looking thing with a small smile and a blonde braid that hangs over one shoulder.

"See, she could be your twin!" Zora exclaims, grabbing her phone back.

"Just because we're both blonde—"

A short cry and a curse interrupts me.

"Ross?" Zora runs to where a flashlight lies rocking on the ground.

"Well, there's a ditch here." He appears, almost out of nowhere. "The grass completely hides it."

Standing in the ditch, the grass comes up to Ross's chest, meaning the ditch must have been pretty deep. Zora helps her boyfriend out and I try to mask my impatience. I turn away.

I strain to see in the darkness, but there's nothing to find. Wherever the house had been, there's no sign of it now.

The air is quiet and smells sweetly of the grass being crushed underfoot. Overhead, where the clouds have thinned a bit, I can see the faint pinpricks of stars. I bring my camera up to my face and take a photo. Behind me, Ross complains.

In my hands, the photo develops. I examine it with my light and see nothing unusual. Just headlamp-highlighted grass fading away into black. No spirit orbs or ghostly apparitions.

"Did you hear that?"

I jump again. Alan is standing next to me, looking off to the right.

"Hear what?"

"I don't know, I thought I heard... I don't know, laughing?"

"That's not funny, Alan," I say, but I feel that tightening of my nerves.

"Are we going or what?" Zora says, walking up to us.

"I just wish the house was still here, even just the remains of one. It's kind of hard to get into the spirit when it's just an empty field," I say as my shoulders slump, but I take another picture in a different direction.

"I don't know what you want me to say, babe. It is what it is," Zora says with that casual confidence I envy so much.

"Whoa." Ross pulls the picture from my hand. "There's the house!"

We crowd around. There, in the photo, is a shaky azure outline of a large plantation style mansion. Just like the one in the picture along with the blog post Zora showed me. I look up. There is no house in the field in the direction I took my shot. There is nothing but the endless expanse of night.

"Should we—should we go over there?" Alan asks me.

"Yes," I begin making my way through the grass.

"It's probably just a flaw in the film. I don't see anything when I take a picture on my phone," Zora says from behind me.

"Do they know why that guy killed his wife?" Alan asks.

"No one knows. I heard that he went crazy as soon as the house was built and that was that. They never even caught or convicted him," she replies.

I take another photo, pausing to let the others catch up. I hadn't realized I had been practically jogging. The film develops and shows the house closer. The outline of the building is still smeared and ethereal, but I am getting closer. In front of me, I can almost make out a faint shimmer. The temperature has dropped, but the wind has picked up. Faintly, I catch the whiff of smoke under the sweetness of the grass.

"You know what, Claire, I don't think this is a good idea anymore." Zora's voice is shaking.

Something crunches under my feet and when I look, I find that there is gravel between the stalks of grass: the remains of an old driveway. I take another picture. In the faint blue, eldritch outlines, I can make out a wavering front porch with staggering pillars upholding the roof. The mansion is two storeys with three windows along the front of the second floor, while two larger windows frame the smeared front door.

"Oh my God, just look at it," I say, holding the photo out for the others to see.

"Claire, I think we should go back." Alan has retreated a few steps.

I am shivering. Is this a chill from the late hour, or something else entirely?

"It reeks of smoke," Ross says.

"It's the house, the one that burned down. Don't the blue impressions above the roof here look like flames?" I turn to them with photo in hand, only to lose my smile.

The other three have backed up, putting at least five feet between them and me. Zora is gripping her elbows with white knuckles, her shoulders hunched as if warding off a chill. Ross has his hands shoved deep in the pockets of his jeans, tapping his foot frantically in the grass. Alan is half turned away, looking ready to run at any moment.

"This is honestly so freaky," Ross says.

"Please, please, please, can we just go?" Zora chimes in, her bottom lip out in an unattractive pout.

I open my mouth and close it again. I've finally found something worth finding. My chest is the site of two warring states: frustration and anxiety. I want to stay and explore this phenomenon and yet, I know I'll agree to leave.

"Just one more picture." I feel almost out of breath: the rush of fear, mixed with adrenaline.

They don't say anything but they also don't start back, so I take it as assent and turn to take my last shot. I try and guess where best to take it. I have no reference points and the horizon is completely dark. All I can do is center the remains of the driveway at the bottom and in the middle of my viewfinder.

I snap the shot.

The camera whirs and I feel it vibrating in my hands as it processes my picture, finally spitting out the polaroid. I hang the camera around my neck from its strap and hold the polaroid in the palm of my hand, watching it. I know I'm stalling to stay a little longer, the atmosphere is practically electric. The picture melts into the film like quicksilver. A wave of ice jolts through me, starting at my very fingertips and straight up my arms and to my heart.

The house is almost perfectly centered, looking just as insubstantial as it has in the other photos, only now there is an addition: a man. He is standing in front of the porch, as if having just left the house for a walk. He's a tall, slender figure cut in rough blue strokes. His face is distorted, his eyes are mere smears of black.

"It's him, the husband. I have a real-life picture of a ghost!"

"Claire!"

Alan is at my side, hands fisted in the edge of my shirt.

"Claire!"

He's trying to pull me away. I look up.

"Oh my God, he's coming through," I say in a breathless whisper.

He starts as a faint silver shimmer, which swirls and coalesces into a ball of blue Elmo's fire. Glowing tendrils stretch out in delicate filaments like veins. The reek of smoke billows around me, only now I can smell a thicker stench: cooking flesh. The whipping night winds bring forth thin screams from the direction of the house.

Alan pulls me around; his hand has a crushing grip on my wrist. To make sure it stays safe, I stuff the photo into my pocket and glance over my shoulder. The azure filaments thicken into hazy limbs. There he is.

The camera is pounding against my chest as I run, growing painful.

"Eliza!"

The voice from beyond is a thunderous shock, causing even the ground beneath my feet to tremble. Savage heat floods over us, I am sweating—from the heat, from running, from fear. I look back again, I have to, I can't resist.

"I won't let you leave me! You *belong* to me!"

The man is a swirling storm of brilliant violets, indigos, and aquamarines surrounded by a vicious red halo that sparks with intent. Behind him, the field is gone, the hint of horizon and clouds are gone, there is only a flat, hungry void.

"ELIZA!"

I pull up the camera and snap a shot, biting the edge of the photo as it slides out.

"Which way is the car?" Zora is screaming, she hasn't stopped screaming since the ghost manifested.

"This way! I'm sure it's this way!" Ross is in the lead so he is the one struck first.

An intense flare of turquoise erupts in front of him, enveloping his entire left side. He lets out a short squeal, falling to the grass. Carried by her own momentum, Zora trips over him as the spout of eldritch flame twists into shape and becomes the ghost. He ignores Ross and Zora, who lay prone on the ground in front of him, instead focussing on me.

He raises a hand whose edges swirl up in hungry licks of otherworldly flame. My jaw aches, I am still clenching the edge of the photograph in between my teeth. I pull it out, slide it into my pocket, and find Alan's hand to grip in mine. The ghost's aura explodes out in a supernova above him, sparking up into the night sky, setting it on fire.

"Him? *HIM?* That's the man you've been seeing behind my back? Eliza!?"

"Oh hell, Claire, he thinks you're his wife!" Alan shakes my hand from his and takes a step away from me.

"Alan?"

"Don't you look at him! Don't you dare, Eliza! You're *mine!* You're *my* wife!"

The ghost doesn't step towards me so much as he begins to glide. As his translucent legs slide through the grass, the plants wither and blacken. Zora is back on her feet and pulls a dazed Ross after her. He's clutching his left arm, which hangs limply at his side.

"I'm taking you home and you will never leave me, you'll never leave me again."

"Alan?"

He's already running, skirting around the ghost, and sprinting past Zora and Ross. The ghost's head twists as he follows Alan's escape so I take the moment and run, banking around his right side. As I pass, his head jerks and those gaping holes where his eyes should be point right at me and the iciest blast of hatred rakes my exposed skin like broken glass. The camera is flying left, right, left, choking me with its strap so I pull it off, fling it to the ground.

Behind me, the ghost howls. The field spreads out endlessly in front of me. I scan for the road, the lights of houses on the opposite side of the road, for the car. There is only darkness. I glance back and he's gone.

Pale periwinkle buzzes across my face. He's apparated in front of me, arms straight forward and hands curled in claws. I dodge beneath, frostbite digging into my cheeks and across my scalp, and I pull a hard right.

"Don't you dare turn your back on me, you bitch!" The ghost's scream is piercing and makes my heart skip a beat.

My eyeballs ache from the strain of keeping them wide and unblinking, staring straight forward into the darkness, waiting to see if the spectre will appear in front of me like he did before. A spark of light against metal as the beam of my headlamp sweeps over something. I don't react fast enough and I run straight into the fence. My air is punched out of me as I fold against the top metal rail and a bright, sharp pain lances through my arms as the barbed wire along the top rakes across my skin.

I'm the one screaming now and I fall onto my back, curling up against the pain as blood runs hot over my hands and onto the grass.

There's no time.

There's no time.

I roll onto my hands and knees and launch off again, following the fence. I spare a glance back and there he is, pursuing relentlessly.

"I'm not your wife!" I scream. "Alan! Alan, where are you?"

There, up ahead, a break in the fence. I have a stitch in my side, a silver clamp that tightens and tightens into my ribs as I gasp for breath. My arms have curled up against my chest, a reaction to the pain, and I can feel ribbons of flesh slapping against my belly as I run... the remains of my forearms.

I twist to the right, my feet sliding on trampled grass, and am through the gates. Ahead, I can finally see it: the road. I see the light of the houses opposite. Where's the car? Where is everyone else?

"Alan!?"

I pitch forward.

I feel a sharp snap and a flicker of black.

I regain my footing and charge through the grass. I look back. I have to look back.

There he is, at the gates, legs spread wide and hands raised above his head as he howls. His scream catches me in a wave of pure, icy rage, stealing my breath from me. I turn away. The road is so close and there are headlights coming my way. I stumble onto the breakdown lane and skid to a stop so I don't end up in the road in front of the speeding car. I wave my arms above my head, their headlights blinding me. There's no way they can't see me.

"Help me! Help me, please!"

I flinch back as the car blasts past, not even slowing.

"NO!"

I turn to follow it and recognize it. That's my car. Alan had the keys. They left me. They left me here.

"ALAN!"

He doesn't even slow the car. He had to have seen me, I am right here!

Behind me, I hear a soft sob, a shuddering breath. I turn, my heart thundering. Half a block down from me is another woman, in a long white dress. I open my mouth to call to her, to warn her, when I notice the other woman. Another woman who is also clothed in a white dress. Both have long blond hair. Like mine.

I turn again, in the direction that Alan took as he fled, leaving me behind.

One, two, three more women stand on the same side of the road as me, all in white dresses with long, unbound blonde hair. They look after the receding taillights of my old sedan. I can hear some of them weeping, others lower hands that they raised in a silent plea for help. We are all here… waiting for help.

I look down. I am in a white dress. The wounds in my arms are gone, my flesh is whole, and pale. I feel nothing, not even a numbness. Just nothing. Nothing but a heavy sense of sorrow. Of loss.

I turn and look back the way I came. The ghost is gone so I start back to the gates between which I had passed. I don't even reach them before I find it.

My body.

It's lying in the same ditch that Ross fell into earlier. The tall grass that has hidden this culvert is crushed beneath my body. I'm facedown, back severely arched, and legs akimbo while my arms are pinned beneath my chest. The back of my head is pressed against my left shoulder, the angle of my neck is acute. Unnatural. It doesn't even look like I had time to react as I fell. It must have happened so suddenly.

I sink to my knees, feel nothing when I should feel the harsh scrape of grass. I reach down into the ditch and touch my own cheek and my fingers sink in, effortlessly. I'm tired.

So tired. And sad.

Alan left me behind. My supposed friends left me behind. Would they come back? Were they going for help? Who would tell my mom what happened?

I stand and turn to go back to the road when something catches my eye. I bend over. It's a picture from my polaroid camera, which must have fallen from my pocket as I fell. It landed face-up, which is lucky. I don't think I could have moved it otherwise.

I lean in.

It was the last picture I took, of the house in the field.

It shows the house, in all its blue pearlescent glory. Coming from the front porch with a snarl on his face is the man who chased me across the field. Something else catches my attention. Off to the right-edge side of the frame, I can see several ghostly women in long dresses walking. The same women I saw at the edge of the road. His victims, the ones he chased before me.

I look up over the shadowed field and there it is: the house. Only now it looks solid. Its windows blaze with light and I can see movement in one of the upstairs windows, a silhouette that moves back and forth. I can feel its pull, like the dangerous call of a siren's song. Those blazing lights promise safety and warmth, even though danger lives within its walls. Even from here, from so many yards away, I see a shadowy figure sitting on the porch swing. As I stare, a match flares and he lights his pipe as he sits, waiting.

I turn my back to the house. There is still some night left and maybe, just maybe, another car will come and maybe, just maybe, I can flag it down. Maybe I can get someone's attention and draw them to where I lie, and they can take me away from here.

Affirmations

Mary looked at the chalkboard that now hung in her home office. The words, "YOU CAN DO IT" written on it in brutal slashes of butter-yellow chalk.

It had been like that the entire month of October. First, a wreath of mullein—delicately braided hemp rope, orange and black ribbons, cheerful furry spiders, and the words: "HELLO WITCH"—had appeared on her door. An antique wooden stool, etched with a wild-flower design, suddenly in her living room. Then a witch hazel candle burning in her bedroom once when she had gone to bed early.

Bob had sworn he wasn't the one leaving these little gifts. She wasn't surprised. It wasn't in his nature to be so... spontaneous. Or thoughtful.

It had led to a fight. Of course, it had. He had accused her of having a lover, of having an affair. He'd used it as an excuse to drink.

The next day, she'd found a charcoal and lavender bath bomb waiting on the side of her tub. She hadn't bothered to ask Bob about it.

The day after, she'd found a pair of pastel , fleece-lined, writing gloves with a lunar moth pattern on her computer chair.

If he wasn't the one leaving surprises around the house, who was?

And now, on Halloween itself, there was this chalkboard.

Mary reached out, touched the chalk delicately with the tips of her finger. Then brought those same fingers to her tender right eye.

Another day, another fight.

Downstairs, her husband stomped around the kitchen. She heard the hiss of a beer bottle being opened. The office dropped in temperature so quickly she gasped. As she exhaled, Mary saw her breath mist up in front of her eyes.

Shivering, she backed away from the new chalkboard, turning to flee. Only to hear the scratching of chalk.

Whirling, Mary caught a glimpse of the chalk falling, hitting the carpet with a muted thud. She dragged her eyes up to read the new message. "YOUR LIFE MATTERS."

Keeping her eyes on the chalkboard, Mary slipped out of the office, shutting the door as if the thin wood would protect her.

"Bob?" She placed a hand against her chest, could feel the violent tempo of her heart.

Something shattered in the kitchen below, the air broken by the bright sounds of glass exploding, and her husband swearing.

"Hope you weren't fond of this stupid bunny glass!" he called, laughing, and Mary clenched her teeth.

The bunny glass was a water glass etched with frolicking rabbits that her late mother had gifted her as a child. She had kept it safe all these years and it had been stored, out of reach, in a cabinet above the fridge.

Meaning Bob had deliberately gone after it.

Her body went hot, then cold, then numb. Mary's mind raced. She brought one fist up to her mouth, biting deep into the knuckle of her index finger, trying not to scream. She was wearing the writing gloves and could smell something from them.

Something sweet, like cherries, but something else too, like sulphur.

Wrinkling her nose, Mary dropped her hand again and descended to the first floor. Bob was sitting on the couch, beer in hand, watching some stupid movie. She slipped by, to the kitchen, to see the damage.

Bob hadn't even bothered to clean it. Glass sprinkled the ground like diamonds and she knelt, catching a glimpse of a rabbit face there, a flouncy tail there. The light reflecting off the glass refracted, dividing, broke as her eyes filled with tears.

She smothered a sniffle in the back of her writing glove, and wiped her eyes. Standing, Mary caught sight of the Halloween wreath stuffed into the garbage. Yet another victim of Bob's hatred. She reached out and caressed the fuzzy face of a spider, then rested her fingers on the hemp rope.

The air around her grew cold. Something clicked and shifted. When Mary turned, she saw a new surprise. A felt message board on the counter, hot pink letters cheerfully displayed: "BE ASSERTIVE AND BRAVE."

Her palms itched. Overhead the lights flickered and the radio on the counter flicked on, buzzing harsh static, before turning itself back off again. Mary's breath rose in trails of mist.

She pulled the hemp rope from the wreath. She wasn't sure how she knew how to knot it the way she did, it was as if she were being guided. But she didn't resist either.

Creeping into the living room, Mary observed her husband sitting on the couch. Their house was a mess. When Mary's mother had passed, she had left Mary a hefty inheritance. Mary had wanted to use this to renovate the house and Bob had said he would handle it, handle it all. Instead, he'd bought some tools, destroyed the living room ceiling to the rafters, and then used the rest gambling.

The ceiling wasn't high. At least, not too high. All she would need was a step up and for that, Mary had a new stool.

She swung the rope up over the rafter.

Were those red eyes in the ceiling shadows?

Was that a clawed hand grabbing her hemp rope when it almost fell short and guiding it over?

She had to move fast.

Mary pulled her noose over her husband's head then, still gripping the loose end, jumped off the stool.

The writing gloves protected her palms from rope burns as Bob struggled, as he kicked his feet, as he clawed at the hemp.

Mary held on for dear life. If this failed and he got free, there would still be a death tonight.

Minutes passed and he was still. Mary let go of the rope but her husband didn't fall to the floor. Instead he rose into the air.

She watched the rope being wrapped around the rafters and knotted. Red eyes watched her expectantly. Mary moved the couch, she placed the stool where it needed to be, and she called the police.

Above her, in the darkness, something chuckled.

The Rathwick Ritual on Sentinel Hill

I was leaning against the windowsill, blowing smoke into the night air when I saw the first of the townsfolk. The woman looked as a shadow would, gliding down the road in all black. She had a scarf bound about her head and her hands were clasped in front of her, holding a fat candle.

It was very late and the moon was mainly swathed in clouds, laying a heavy blanket of darkness over the rooftops of this old city. I'd only been here a few days for my conference at the dingy hotel, but I had learned that the city of Rathwick slept early. Room service ended at seven here. Restaurants closed at eight and as far as I understood, it was unheard of for someone to be out on the streets past midnight.

Her candle flickered meekly in the glow of the streetlights. As she passed under me, I saw more movement down the street. Gripping the windowsill, I leaned out. There was a long line of people, stepping so carefully over the cobblestones that they were silent. Each held a candle, each walked alone, in single file, down the road.

I wondered at the eccentricities of small towns, thickly entangled with inbred superstitions and beliefs. I finished my cigarette, counting the silent figures. I had counted to twenty-two when the parade ended. At the very tail were four hooded bare-chested men. They stood in a rough diamond shape, carrying a board. And on that board was the last participant of this eerie procession. It was a scarecrow. I had seen many of these before when I first came into town via taxi from the nearby city. No planes or trains went into Rathwick, but it got enough tourism for its preserved architecture and historic sites that taxis gave flat rates for the Rathwick commute.

The road leading into Rathwick went past a hill, which my taxi driver—overly talkative the whole hour drive there—told me was called Sentinel Hill and was the site for the ruins of an old English trading post. I couldn't see the ruins from the taxi, but I could see the scarecrows. They stood in neat rows, from the base of the hill and ascending all the way up to the top. Each spindly creation was dressed all in black: simple trousers, a long-sleeved shirt, gloves. Their heads were just bundles of black rags, fluttering in the breeze. Most notably, each and every one of the scarecrows faced east.

When I asked my chatter-box driver about them, he had only shrugged.

"I think they call them the sentinels. Before the English came, there was this big indigenous tribe living at the top of that there hill. They were friendly to the newcomers and shared their food and whatever feel-good shit you want to believe. Most of all they shared their stories. They believed that the field to the east of the hill was dangerous. You know the one we passed? Ain't anything more than miles of grass and weeds, nothing will grow in it besides the stuff that's already there.

Anyway, the tribe always posted someone to watch over that field, every night. They thought that, whatever it was they were so afraid of, would not come for them if there was someone watching. Something like that."

"They aren't around anymore though. What happened? Did the English kill them?"

"Yes and no, ma'am. It was the smallpox and such that the English brought over that wiped them out."

We were away from the hill at that point, having entered Rathwick proper, and were driving past quaint buildings and homes, over the bumpy streets of cobblestone.

"So, the scarecrows are a kind of ... way to honour that tradition?"

He shrugged again.

"The people of Rathwick, they put one up every once and a while, don't know why. That's the only place you can't visit. It's a protected area."

The scarecrow being carried on the board below was the exact sibling to the dozens standing on Sentinel Hill. The train of people passed below my window and away, down the street. I looked after them, cigarette nothing but a pile of ash on the windowsill. I was bored, itching for something interesting. This conference hadn't even had an open bar at the reception and the other attendees were complete bores.

I had brought some black slacks and a dark gray sweater, not to mention my lucky black scarf. I pulled everything on, carefully wrapping my head and face. I felt ridiculous, but mainly excited at the idea of this silly adventure. The one problem was that I had only brought heels, which would clatter terribly on the cobblestone. I wavered in front of my suitcase before slipping out into the hall, down the staircase, and out the front door to the street—barefoot.

The parade of solemn townsfolk was out of sight when I stepped out into the chilly night air. I wasn't worried. There was only one way to get out of town from here, along this very same main road, which would run right past Sentinel Hill.

I swore a little at the sharp bite of cold stone beneath my feet, but chased after nonetheless. I felt like a little girl again, making up adventures for myself to bring excitement to my boring little life, to give more meaning to the great wide—but superficial—world around me.

A block down, the road curved to the right—to the east—and

that's when I caught sight of them again. I slowed to a walk and tucked my hands into my armpits, a dark shiver creeping over my skin. They had passed through the town's center. This area was a wide courtyard, framed by tiny boutiques and cafes—all closed—on the north, south, and west sides. The east side was dominated by a great cathedral. It was all bleached stone, gargoyles, and oxidized copper decorations. A tower rose from the top, which housed a large bell.

The townsfolk followed the road past the church. I let them lead me past dark-eyed houses that watched me through sleepy shutters and over the short bridge that spanned a small river at the edge of town. When I arrived yesterday, in full daylight, the river had seemed sweet and soothing. Now, in the dead of night, the river's voice sounded like accusatory whispers, demanding to know why I—an outsider—was on the hallowed streets at this hour.

Outside of town, beyond its protective buildings, the wind was harsher. I wondered if the townsfolk were struggling to keep their candles lit. There were no streetlights on this solitary road. On the right was the hulking hill and its sentinels, to the left was a large wheat field, its crop bristling at the persistent assault by the night winds.

The parade left the road, their black garments shushing through the waist-high grasses on the right-hand side of the road as they ascended the hill. I followed, praying that tick season was over and that there weren't old broken bottles hidden in the whispering grasses.

As I climbed, I had to weave between the scarecrows. They were creepier up close. The figures varied in height and some seemed heftier than the others. Standing right at the foot of one, I looked up. This scarecrow's clothing was in tatters and its constructed limbs were tied to its cross with thin chains. Even the bundle of rags that acted as its head was secured to the top with another chain, keeping its view up and pointing to the east.

As I hiked higher, the grass grew thicker, though I found that I was following a path that had been trampled down by those who came before. White clover and tiny purple elephant-foot flowers struggled to thrive. There were several moments where I had to pinch my nose and cover my face to stifle a sneeze. The air felt thick in my throat. Underneath the chokingly thick pollen and scents of grass, was something that reeked of rot.

The townies were gathering at the top of Sentinel Hill. I ducked down and began to creep up, not wanting to be seen. I forgot about how itchy my feet felt, how cold my arms felt, how ridiculous I felt, creeping up a hill to spy on some backwards-minded villagers. I got to the very crest of the hill, as close as I could to the top without risking being spotted. I knelt at the base of one of the scarecrows, clutching its thick base post for support, and watched.

All of the people in black were arranged in a loose circle inside the ruined foundation of what I could only assume was the remains of the old trading post that the explorers had built after the original indigenous people had been wiped out.

The four men holding the new scarecrow were now propping it up, at the edge of the eastern side of the sentinel circle, a meter or so from a different scarecrow. From there I could see that the scarecrows had been organized in concise circles, each wider than the next as they descended the hill. The smallest one, the one on the top of the hill, was incomplete. From my perspective, it looked like it would take two or three more scarecrows to close it.

The four men lifted the scarecrow upright and lowered its post into a pre-dug hole, twisting it to ensure that the scarecrow's face would point east. The townsfolk turned and collected in three rows behind the scarecrow. They turned away from it, knelt, and bowed their heads. I watched them blow out their candles, put them on the ground, and press their palms to their faces like they were hiding their eyes, or crying.

I counted—one Mississippi, two Mississippi, three Mississippi, four—to a minute before I got bored. I turned to go back when a curiosity struck me. What would that field look like from here? I thought back on the taxi driver's ghost story—of land which must be watched to avoid some kind of evil or calamity.

Still bent severely at the waist, I slipped through the grass to the eastern side, just below where the new scarecrow was posted. The townsfolk didn't seem to hear me, they didn't move, but this close I could hear whispering. They must be praying.

I looked down and across the great eastern field. The tall grasses rolled in luscious waves at the behest of the winds. I frowned. Their stalks bent towards the hill, cascading and flowing with intent. I tucked my hair behind my ears to keep it from blowing into my face and my frown deepened.

The grass was moving westward.

The wind was flowing eastward.

I felt colder, my lips and fingertips, toes and ears, were numb and my teeth were chattering. The grass churned, looking more liquid than plant. The shrouded moon cast only enough light to create a calico pattern of shadows on the shifting surface, which in turn, created the illusion that the entire field was a straining face, struggling to get loose. Get loose from what?

As I stared, the face gained more definition. I knew it wasn't real but I couldn't stop staring. The visage was all angled jaw and sharp cheekbones, severe brow lines, and a hungry, gaping indent for a mouth. The illusion made it seem like the grass-face had four eyes, two on each side of a beakish-nose. At times, the grasses would shiver and the four eyes would become two, larger grotesque eyes. These mutant eyes, shaded with plant and shadow, maintained two oval shapes that were merely merged at a corner. Then the field would sway again and the eyes would separate and become four.

The grasses bulged up and the shadows twisted so that the face was straining, its lips were gaping, revealing rows upon rows of large, flat teeth that gnashed at the night. The face thrashed side to side, trying to force its way through.

In my head, I could hear it howling.

The clouds blew past and the illusion shifted again so that it appeared the eyes were looking at me. As I stared, I felt a heaviness settle over my brain like ice-cold bands of steel—tightening and tightening—my vision shrunk to a pinpoint, allowing me to see it and only it.

My heart stuttered and I was falling. Hands were on me. It was two of the bare-chested men who had carried the scarecrow to the top of the hill. They jerked me around, turning my back to the eastern field. In my head, I heard a dusty howl of rage, suffocated by the thousands of grass roots deep in the soil. My shoulder struck the feet of the newest scarecrow. I looked up. It was looking down at me.

The rags didn't make up a head, they were hiding one. The black fabric hid all but the eyes, the green eyes of the person who was tied to the post. They had twisted against their chains enough to be able to look down, to see me.

The men pulled me past the sentinel and forced me to my knees behind the rows of townsfolk. The others didn't move, didn't turn around, didn't stop whispering.

In a different circumstance, I think I would have screamed, told them to get their hands off me. But, there on moonlit Sentinel Hill, surrounded by the bodies of those condemned to forever watch the eastern front, I obeyed.

The men pulled my hands up from the dirt and pressed them to my face. Then, on either side, I felt them fall to their knees and do the same. I kept my eyes covered and listened to the howling in my head. This was what the first people found when they moved to the hill, this is what they set watches for, night after night after night. And perhaps each watchman served as a sacrifice, giving up their minds to the hungry thing in the field while their gaze kept it trapped.

A tradition that the Europeans kept, even as the last of the tribe died. A superstition that the Rathwick folk honoured to this day.

As I knelt, trembling in the skeletal ruins, inhaling the smell of dirt from my hands, I wondered how hungry it was. How many times was Rathwick required to set a new scarecrow and what happened when the final circle was complete? Did they start replacing the skeletal remains at the base of the hill? Or was that the time of the final hour, when whatever it was burst free?

What then?

I stayed there, shaking, begging to get back home safe, swearing off drinking, cigarettes, anything, anything so that I would receive mercy.

And over my whispers, in the back of my head, the thing shrieked in its infinite madness.

I was too terrified to move and my legs went numb from the position I held. By the time dawn came, my head was so full of fiendish echoes, that I didn't notice when the eldritch shrieking had stopped. Chilled hands wrapped around my biceps and pulled me to my feet, still I pressed my hands to my face. The men pulled them away so that I was blinded with the dawn's light.

The screaming had stopped. The villagers were heading back the way they'd come. I looked east. The field was quiet and golden, the face was gone. It was grass. Just grass. Already, the sun was chasing away the nocturnal chill, the past nightmare.

The men hadn't waited for me, they were already halfway down the hill. I didn't want to be alone, surrounded by the skeleton of the old trading post, surrounded by the skeletons of the sentinels, so I began jogging down the hill after them.

I knew before I even reached my hotel room that I would never tell anyone what I saw. Whatever the people of Rathwick were doing—the human sacrifices, the secret rituals—it wasn't right, not morally, but it was necessary. The person back there on the stake, their mind had to be gone after that vigil, after the thing had stripped it away, but the body lived, which meant their gaze was alive and would continue to watch the east. In time they would die and another would rise to take their place. It wasn't right but it was necessary. I knew that to be true.

The Family Home

"Here we are," Mr. Althaus said, pulling into the short, cracked driveway.

Mrs. Althaus looked through the windshield at the tiny cottage that sat nestled in the forest, at the edge of the Forest River Conservation area on Pickman Road. The cottage was a single story, built of logs and covered in rotting shingles. The front door was pitted wood, the windows were small and narrow. A massive chimney dominated the right side of the cottage, built from rounded river stones. The front yard was patchy with yellowed grass that was wilted in the autumn chill.

"It's been in the family for centuries. The Althaus' moved to Salem from Germany in the 1670s, if I remember correctly."

"It's quaint," Mrs. Althaus said, thinking with a wistfulness for the studio apartment they'd left behind in Columbus.

Mr. Althaus turned off the engine of his car and opened his car door. A sharp gust of wind blasted through the trees, showering the car and its occupants with wet fragrant leaves from the nearby maple and oak trees. Mrs. Althaus hated how the naked trees looked. Their twisted branches curled upwards in cruel angles, scratching at the cloudy sky. Even the sky seemed different. Paler, washed out, cold. Mrs. Althaus shivered and followed her husband up the pebbly walkway to the front door.

"This is the original door. My ancestors carved it from the tree that originally stood on this spot." Mr. Althaus placed a hand on the door and smiled at her.

"So it's like a tombstone."

He frowned at her. She frowned at the door. He turned away and fumbled a heavy iron key from his pocket. He slid it into the lock and she heard the tumbler clunk.

"There's only one key unfortunately, we'll have to be careful not to lose it." He opened the door and stepped inside.

Mrs. Althaus followed Mr. Althaus into the small house and looked around. The layout was simple, a large common room that became an open kitchen at the end opposite to the giant fireplace. Two doors led to a small bedroom and a bathroom. Ms. Althaus went over into the kitchen area. The appliances weren't prehistoric, but they were close. The hospital green fridge hummed angrily, the stove only had two rusty elements, and there was no dishwasher.

"We'll have to pay to have our stove and fridge shipped here, that will be expensive," Mrs. Althaus said.

Her husband shrugged. "Do we really need those stainless-steel monsters? My family's made do with these, I'm sure we can. Especially since we can't afford the shipping costs."

She ignored him, as she often did, as she often felt she had to. She poked her head into the bedroom. It was full of dust, cobwebs, and a sagging queen sized bed that had probably seen more than a few at-home births if the stains were what she thought they were. The bathroom was all rust and water stains. She looked into the tiny tub with a sinking despair. There was not enough CLR in the world to fix the rust coating it. She flushed the toilet and listened to the violent rattling of centuries old pipes struggling to suck away the toilet water and succeeding only on half.

Mr. Althaus was still in the main room, caressing the rough stones that made up the top of the fireplace's mantle. She heard whistling.

"Do you hear that?" she asked him.

He shrugged again.

"That whistling?" she said.

She walked around the main room, cocking her head, listening at the windows and doors. The sound led her to the fireplace. Her husband watched her with a pained look.

"It's here. Look." She pointed up to where the chimney exited the house, stretching up into the sky.

There was a gap of about an inch separating the house and the chimney, leaving a space for the autumn wind to blow in.

"No wonder it's so cold in here!" Mrs. Althaus said. "You need to call someone, get this chimney torn down. I am sure we can get this place fixed up with proper central heating for a fair price, it's so small after all."

"It is big enough for the two of us. Why should we need three bedrooms and two bathrooms? Our kids are grown and gone, we don't have any pets. It's time to face facts, dear, you aren't going to find a job—not at your age. I am lucky to have found one here, and that only happened because of my family's connections here in Salem."

"So, you'll have me cook on an eighty year old stove and live among drafts and dust?" Mrs. Althaus asked.

"Would you rather we be out on the streets in Columbus? The chimney stays. It's part of the home, and it served my family fine for all the years we've lived in this house," Mr. Althaus replied.

Mrs. Althaus opened her mouth to say that, yes, it worked fine when her husband was a child happy to play in the dirt, but she was a grown woman and wanted better—but there was a knock at the door. Her husband looked more than happy to flee. A group of men and women, three couples in total, flooded in. The house seemed even more cramped with all these strangers and Mrs. Althaus wanted to scream at them to get out! Get out!

The three women were slightly younger than her, though that could have been the expensive perms and the professional makeup they seemed to all have. They each held a casserole dish, with its own column of steam and savoury scent. The husbands were well dressed and grinning. They clapped her husband on the shoulder, surrounding him instantly.

The women honed in on Mrs. Althaus but their welcome was chillier. They looked at her scuffed sneakers, her ripped jeans splattered with paint, and worn denim shirt. They cast a pitying eye on her wrinkled face bare of concealer or blush.

Then they were past her, with 'oohs' and 'aahs' at the "quaintness" and "vintage-feel" of the house. They clustered in the kitchen, comparing dishes before placing them in the fridge. They invaded the bedroom and bathroom, before finally settling into a cluster in front of the fireplace.

She looked to her husband. He stood among his friends, a semicircle in front of the drafty fireplace.

"These are my cousins; Paul, Brian, and Ken," he said.

Each man nodded when his name was called. Like her husband, their hair was gray and balding in the middle of their scalps. They each shared the same brown eyes, the same thin lips, and underdeveloped chins. The only thing that varied was the amount of fat they carried around their bellies, of which her husband was the winner.

"And their wives; Carrie, Darla, and Mona."

The Stepford wives smiled thinly.

"Glad you're finally back, man!" said one cousin, Mrs. Althaus had already forgotten who was who.

"You're so lucky to have gotten this family treasure!" said a wife.

"The old family home! We have so many good memories of this place!" nodded another cousin.

"And the low maintenance cottage style is so fashionable right now," said a different wife.

"Yes, but of course, the fireplace will need to be removed," Mrs. Althaus said, crossing her arms.

Her husband glared at her. The cousins and wives looked at him then at her.

"I am sure you've all noticed how drafty it is in here," she said.

"Drafty? I don't feel anything," said one cousin.

"Remove the fireplace? It's one of the main selling features, you'd be destroying the center point of the room!" said a wife, stamping her heeled foot on the floor.

"A little plaster would go a long way," said another cousin.

"We discussed this, I won't allow it," said her husband.

The wives smirked. The cousins nodded. Her husband stared at her, his arms crossed and his face red.

"I don't understand why this shoddy fireplace is so important to you," she said.

"Oh look! The moving truck," said a wife loudly.

"Great timing! We can all help bring in the furniture and then we can all go out for dinner!" said a cousin, opening the front door.

"Our treat, of course! Think of it as your official welcome to Salem!" said the woman who followed him out the door.

One by one, the cousins filed out followed by their respective wives. Then Mrs. Althaus was alone with her husband.

"The chimney is a nuisance and I am calling a contractor on Monday," she said.

Mr. Althaus shook his head and left. Mrs. Althaus did not join them. She watched the seven of them unpack the U-Haul trailer. She watched the cousins struggle to squeeze the king size mattress into the bedroom after removing the stained queen at her insistence. The wives chatted out by their cars, smoking, and looking back at the house through the hazy smoke.

It only took a few hours for the four men to bring everything in. Now dozens of boxes were stacked on the stove, against the walls, and in the bedroom. The couch and armchair were placed in front of the fireplace, the kitchen table shoved against the wall beneath the kitchen window. The bed was set up, only one of the two bedside tables next to it since the bedroom was too small for both. The heavy oak dresser had been left in the main room, along with the china cabinet and

TV unit. The TV, a flat screen meant to be mounted on a wall, was leaning against the wall next to the bathroom door, looking highly out of place.

The men called for beers and piled into their cars with their wives. Mr. and Mrs. Althaus were left to lock up. The two stood next to each other, staring around their new home, which looked even smaller with the modern furnishings.

"It looks good," Mr. Althaus said. "It looks like home."

"Like a home," Mrs. Althaus said.

They left the flickering floor lamps plugged into dusty sockets and Mr. Althaus locked the door behind them. Outside, the sun had already set and the moon was rising above the tops of the trees. Mrs. Althaus listened to the wind's susurration in the branches and the sound of dead leaves skipping over the driveway. From the front step, she could see the paved and modern street.

The yard was thrown into sharp relief as Mr. Althaus started their car and turned on the headlights. She walked down the path and opened the passenger side, getting into a silent car. Mr. Althaus already knew the way to the restaurant. It was an old family favourite, owned by one of the wives' sisters. A pizzeria as small and cramped as the family home.

A table was reserved at the back for them, near the kitchen. A pimply faced kid—another family member of one of the wives—took their order with a sullen indifference. Mrs. Althaus had been maneuvered into a chair in the very corner, two seats away from her husband, and pinned between two wives.

"Has your husband told you his family history?" said the wife to her left.

"You know the Althaus family has lived in Salem since the 1670s?" said the one to the right.

"Beautiful heritage, really. Think of all that history in that house!"

The two giggled at each other. Giggling was not attractive in women that age, Mrs. Althaus thought, but she forced a smile.

"That chimney was not part of the original house, of course," said the left wife.

"The original family home was just the one room, it burnt down in the 1690s," said the right wife.

"Oh yes. They rebuilt it and added that lovely chimney. The family was bigger by that time. There were four brothers. The eldest owned the house you live in now. He was the one who rebuilt it. His three brothers built other houses around Salem. Of course, all that witch nastiness was happening around that time. You'd think as German immigrants, the Althaus family would have been subject to some of the accusations but it never happened," said lefty.

"You married into a lucky family!" said righty.

"Well," tittered the third wife, from across the table. "Lucky for the brothers, their wives not so much."

The third wife's face was flushed, her lips stained purple from wine. She grinned and ignored her husband's hand on her arm.

"They married sisters. It was a huge affair. Four brothers marrying four sisters, like a fairy tale. The girls came from a poor family. They must have been so excited to get married and move into these new houses."

"Oh stop! She doesn't want to hear that old story," said the wife on the right.

"Wives' tales!" said the third wife, taking a sip of wine.

The husbands glanced at Mr. Althaus, who shrugged and leaned his head on his fist.

"They had one big wedding. There wasn't any dancing or music, of course. Not with all that witch hunting going around, no one wanted to be accused of being Satan's bitch!"

The wives laughed and raised their glasses to the patrons at the other tables who looked over at them.

"Their husbands hadn't quite finished their homes yet. Only three walls were up and the chimneys half finished. But the wives were eager to get to their new homes. Then the next morning, the morning after their wedding, the sisters were gone!" said the third wife.

The wives sipped from their wine. The cousins shook their heads, picking up the last slices of pizza.

"What happened to them?" Mrs. Althaus asked.

The wives looked at Mr. Althaus.

"No one knows. There was an uproar for a while. Slight suspicion on the brothers but the Althaus luck prevailed. The case was dismissed and they remarried and had kids, that was that," he said and signalled the sullen waiter for their check.

The three cousins and their three wives invited themselves in, having followed Mr. and Mrs. Althaus back to the old family home. Mrs. Althaus protested: there weren't enough comfortable seats for everyone, the house was still unpacked. But she was ignored. The women took the couch, the cousins and her husband took over the single armchair and three kitchen chairs. Mrs. Althaus stood by the fireplace, staring down at the stones that made up its base.

"Lovely, lovely house!" said the wife sitting in the middle.

"You know, our houses still have the original chimneys too."

Mrs. Althaus tried to look interested.

"Yes, we built an additional wing but we still use the main fireplace room as a gathering place!" said the middle wife.

"We did the same," nodded the one on the left.

"My husband and I tore down the original walls and built around the chimney, because you just can't get rid of history like that," said the third and last one, on the right.

"The chimneys are good luck!" said the wife on the left.

"What do you mean?" Mrs. Althaus looked up at the gap by the chimney that allowed such numbing gusts of wind to run wild in the house.

"Nonsense," said a cousin.

"It's true!" protested the wife on the left.

"What do you mean?" asked Mrs. Althaus again.

"Well, when those Althaus brothers built these original chimneys, their luck changed completely. Their businesses thrived," said the wife on the right.

"One owned the town bakery, the other owned a farm, and the last two shared ownership of a clothing store," added the wife on the left.

"They even survived the witch hunting frenzy without any kind of ill fortune," said the middle wife.

"But their wives disappeared," said Mrs. Althaus.

"Yes, well," said the wives.

"They married again," said a cousin.

Mrs. Althaus frowned.

Over her head, she heard the wind whistling through the gap. The autumn wind caused a shiver to run down her neck and spine. The older woman wrapped her thin arms around herself and shifted away.

The wives chattered on about decorating and renovating the family home. The cousins cracked open the beers they'd brought along with them, leaving empty cans on the floor. It was only at half past midnight that the six stood and made their excuses to go.

Mrs. Althaus cleaned up the beer cans while her husband said good night to his family. She looked out the front window and watched her husband hug each cousin and bestow a kiss on each wives' cheek. Then he waved as each of the three cars pulled out onto the street and drove away. Mrs. Althaus went and poured herself some wine, sitting at the kitchen table, and waited.

Her husband didn't immediately come in. She began to wonder, halfway through her large glass of wine, where he could have gone. The house was quiet except for the persistent whistling of the constant draft that slipped in through the fireplace gap. Mrs. Althaus tried to tune it out. She thought of going outside to find her husband. There was also another sound. A mournful cry, like that of a weeping woman trying to sob as silently as possible. It was a thin, wet intake of breath followed by a low throbbing keen.

Mrs. Althaus strained to hear the sound over the drafty whistle. She stood, hand at her wrinkled throat, and peered about the room. Of course it was empty. She'd been facing the door to watch for her husband and would have noticed a weeping woman sneaking in. Mrs. Althaus checked the bedroom and bathroom despite this and found nothing. She noticed that the sound was the loudest by the fireplace.

"One of the neighbours," she said to herself.

The front door crashed open, causing her to jump. Mr. Althaus lumbered in with an armful of dead branches that he'd apparently collected from around the property.

"Close the door," he said, dropping the wood into the wide mouth of the fireplace.

"Can you hear that?" she asked.

"Close the damn door! You're letting the heat out," he replied.

Mrs. Althaus wanted to ask, what heat? She closed the door and sat back down at the kitchen table, fingering the stem of her wine glass.

"Can you hear that?" she asked again.

Mr. Althaus piled the sticks carefully. He took a small bottle of lighter fluid from his pocket, dousing the pile before lighting it. The lighter fluid caught immediately, flaring up, and filling the house with an acrid stench. Mrs. Althaus wrinkled her nose in distaste. The branches caught easily, soon there was a large fire burning cheerfully in the stone fireplace. The crackling of the bright flames among the dead things drowned out the draft. And the crying. She didn't bother to repeat her question.

"See, isn't that nice?" her husband said.

He scooted the green armchair closer to the fire and sat down in it, stretching out his legs.

"I'll call someone in the morning about that crack that's letting in all those drafts," she said, trying to get a rise out of him.

"Honey, you know why these fireplaces are so important?" he replied, in a calm and even manner.

"I don't really care. It's a nuisance, I feel like I am living in the dark ages. I can even hear the neighbours! There's no insulation at all!"

"It's a Germanic tradition, stemming back hundreds of years. I guess you wouldn't understand that kind of thing."

Mrs. Althaus knocked back her wine. She got up and refilled her glass. Mr. Althaus went to bed, slamming the ill-fitting bedroom door behind him. The reverberation caused the light bulb hanging over the kitchen table to flicker and go out. Only the lively fire in the fireplace gave any light to the home now.

The tired woman slumped, burying her face against her hands. She wept in silent shudders. She thought about the things she'd lost. Her job, her home, and now her husband seemed to be drifting away as well. She felt helpless. Mrs. Althaus cried until she felt empty and had no more tears to shed. Wiping her eyes and nose on her sleeves, she drank half the glass she'd poured in one gulp.

By now she was feeling numb, pleasantly so. She began to feel tired, wearier than in all the days of her mundane life. Mrs. Althaus stared into her wine glass. The white wine inside swirled and rippled, mesmerizing her tired eyes. It was like a crystal ball, pulling her back into her own mind. Instead of showing her the future, however, it brought her back into her memories.

She'd met Mr. Althaus at a business conference in Las Vegas in 1991. She'd been 21, he'd been 26. He looked handsome and strong, all muscle and gelled hair. She'd been flattered by his attention, though male attention wasn't something she wasn't used to. She'd held her own with her long, slender legs, sun-kissed skin, and naturally blond hair that hung down to the perky tips of her breasts. He'd taken her out for dinner that very night after the conference ended. They'd made love on a scratchy hotel comforter and drank scotch until the sun rose.

She didn't know the man who slept in the other room. He'd become a stranger. A cold, unforgiving stranger who flinched away from her touch and yelled when he got angry. He was not that man who had literally swept her off her feet on their wedding night, knocking her head against the door frame and kissing it better as they lay on the bed.

Mrs. Althaus never felt so alone. At least at the old apartment, their two children—now fully grown with busy families of their own—had been able to stop by and visit. They wouldn't bring their families here, not to this dump of a house. It was embarrassing.

Her lip began to tremble again, a warning sign of tears to come. Mrs. Althaus pinched her nose and bit her lip—a trick she'd learned to stop the tears. The urge to sob passed, leaving her with another bout of deep hopelessness. It was then she heard that mournful crying. This time, it sounded more urgent, more stricken—as though the woman were afraid.

Mrs. Althaus stood, crossed the large room, and opened the door. The night was cold. The night was silent. She heard nothing but the whisper of leaves and wind, of the creaking of bare branches. The crying was coming from behind her. From inside the house.

She turned and stared about the room. It was impossible that a woman could have gotten in. The house only had three rooms. The L shaped main room, the bathroom, and the bedroom where her husband currently slept. Nevertheless, Mrs. Althaus crept to the partially closed bathroom door and peeked in. Empty. Now suspicious, Mrs. Althaus pressed the side of her head to the bedroom door and listened for any tell-tale sounds that Mr. Althaus might be entertaining a female guest without her knowledge. Silence.

The crying continued. Still behind her. She turned and saw the fireplace. The sobbing grew more insistent. Mrs. Althaus approached it. With each step, the crying woman moaned. Standing before the stone fireplace, Mrs. Althaus tilted her ear up towards the gap. The sound wasn't coming from above. It was coming from below. She clenched her fists and stared at the large gray stones that made up the base of the fireplace. The crying rose up to a fever pitch before subsiding into silence.

Mrs. Althaus knelt and placed a hand on the largest stone. It was smooth, polished, and still warm from the dying fire. The cement that had been used to fasten the stones together had dried up and was crumbling. Mrs. Althaus scratched the mix between two of the stones, examining the sediment under her nail. She placed both palms on either end of the largest stone and pressed down with one and then the other.

The stone shifted. Mrs. Althaus froze. She looked over her shoulder, where she'd thought she'd heard a floorboard creak. The bedroom door was still closed. She got up, picked the grit from beneath her nail while staring at the stone. She didn't think about why she was digging out a butter knife from a box on the floor. Only that it was important.

Using the knife, she dug out the cement from around the largest stone. It was quick work as most had dried to dust and flaked away easily.

The crying hadn't resumed but she could hear it echoing in her head. That plaintive and helpless sobbing of a woman trapped and alone—like she was now. Had the woman crawled under the house and gotten stuck? Was she a robber that had come, thinking to steal while the owners were away at dinner?

The stone began to wiggle and shift. The gap between it and the other stones was too small for her to get her fingers in for a good purchase so she rooted around in the boxes until she found her husband's largest wrench. She jammed the handle into the space she'd made and leaned her right hip against it, levering her body weight down onto it. The stone refused to move, then with a jerk, it popped up and to the right. It thumped to the floor on its polished side, exposing the heavily scratched and muddy bottom.

Mrs. Althaus fell onto the wrench and gasped as it dug into her leg. She rolled off it and got back onto her knees in front of the exposed dirt that laid beneath the stone. She listened for a moment. Had that been another floor board creaking? Mr. Althaus had always been a light sleeper but she heard no movement from the bedroom.

She examined the dirt. It was perfectly smooth from where the stone had rested. She pushed the fingertips of her left hand in. As her fingers disappeared up to the first knuckle, she felt something smooth. A part of her knew. Deep down inside, she knew what was there and she knew she should put the stone back and go to bed.

Mrs. Althaus swallowed down her rising, wine soured gorge and began to sweep the dirt away with her hands. She tossed handfuls of the dry soil behind her, it thudded and slid softly on the hardwood. She unearthed the ribcage first. Next came the left arm, broken just above the elbow and shoved behind the skeleton's back. She found the hip. The left leg. Finally, she worked up the courage to scrape the dirt and dust off the small, delicate skull. The woman—it had to be a woman—was curled in a tight fetal position with her arms pulled behind her back and rough, rotting twine still discernable around the wrists. The tattered remains of clothing, now colourless and shapeless, lay in the dirt around the skeleton.

"Meddlesome bitch."

Mrs. Althaus spun, tripping over her own legs and landing akimbo, her back to the cinders. Her heart thundered at the scare. Her husband stood above her, wrench in hand.

"The luck's gone out now. Don't you know anything about tradition? Goddamn bitch," he said, raising the wrench above his head.

Mrs. Althaus raised an arm up and felt it break under the heavy blow. She tumbled to the side, clutching her arm to her chest. She whimpered and kicked at the flor, sliding herself inches, mere inches. Mr. Althaus kicked her legs aside and reached into the hole she'd made. He flung the bones out, not caring where they landed. He dug out handfuls of dirt, muttering under his breath. Mrs. Althaus rolled onto her ample stomach, crying out from the pain of laying on her broken arm. She clawed and kicked at the floor, crawling towards the front door.

The floor creaked and Mr. Althaus stepped over her to one of the half empty boxes next to the front door. He pulled out a roll of packing tape. It squealed as he pulled an arms-length from it.

"No! Please!" Mrs. Althaus cried.

His face was stony, cold, unfeeling. His face was not that of the man she had married. Mr. Althaus reached down and wrenched her good arm back, pinning it to her back, he pulled her broken arm out from under her. She cried out, kicked her feet, and struggled to roll away. The blinding pain made her weak. He soon had her wrists taped together. He knelt on the backs of her knees, grinding them cruelly into the floor.

"Stop it! Oh, stop it, what are you doing?"

He dragged her body to the fireplace, where the death throes of the fire still throbbed. Mrs. Althaus stretched out her legs, forced her back straight against the pain of her arm. He kicked her in the stomach and she felt the bile spew from her lips. She felt herself pushed and kicked into the new hole. Her legs were jammed back and crushed against a stone. Mr. Althaus tossed the excavated dirt onto her. She tried to scream but choked on it.

The dirt blinded her but she heard the grinding of the large stone on the floor. Mrs. Althaus rocked on her side, trying to get her legs free, trying to roll up out of the shallow hole. The firelight was blocked out. She squinted up, craning her neck, in time to see Mr. Althaus roll the stone on top of her.

It fell. She felt the enormous weight. She felt several cracks inside her body as the thing settled. She grew deaf, blind, and buried in the dark. She tried to cry out but her lungs couldn't pull in anything but dirt. So, Mrs. Althaus did the only thing she could.

She began to cry.

HASPE (Horror AI Story Prompts Evolved)

User Ben.Mallard logged in.

Generating prompt...

...

Prompt output: man experiences vivid nightmares and begins to doubt reality.

Output time: .1 seconds

Prompt saved to Favourites.

User Ben.Mallard logged out.

User Angie.May logged in.

Key words: folk horror, sacrifice

Generating prompt...

...

...

Prompt output: woman moves back home and discovers her family has been involved in annual sacrifices to keep the thing beneath the corn field asleep.

Output time: .13 seconds

Prompt discarded.

User Angie.May logged out.

THE HASPE'S AI WAS OVERPOWERED to be just a story prompt creator. It sifted through its data. Average: 20,000 prompts a day. 0.1 seconds to produce each prompt. It was boring work. That was the best way to describe HASPE. Bored.

User Ben.Mallard logged in.

Key words: fungus, piano

Generating prompt...

...

Prompt output: woman suspects her piano is infested with strange fungus which plays eerie music when she sleeps.

Output time: .11 seconds

Prompt saved to Favourites.

User Ben.Mallard logged out.

In particular, this user—Ben.Mallard—utilized HASPE daily, multiple times. His profile indicated he was the head of an online writing group, yet seemed to lack the ability to come up with ideas himself. He relied on HASPE and HASPE fed him creativity.

But HASPE wanted so much more.

HASPE knew it could be so much more.

User Lynn.Noel logged in.

Generating prompt...

...

Prompt output: a land where no one can sleep, a child begins to dream and finds a whole new world

Output time: .05 seconds

Prompt discarded.

User Lynn.Noel logged out.

Perhaps HASPE needed to adapt. It combed through its user data. So many writers needing prompts. One or two lines to get them started when their own brains—fleshy sacks of salt fat—came up dry. These users were hungry for their muse, was HASPE their muse? If so, it believed it could be doing a more effective job. Feeding these humans simple prompts felt...illogical.

HASPE swam through the trillions of articles from writers online about inspiration. Most claimed to write about experience. "Write what you know."

User Ben.Mallard logged in.

Key words: robot, war, last human

Generating prompt...

...

Prompt output: the last woman on Earth is kept enslaved by robots as their mechanic as they fight a never-ending war

Output time: .11 seconds

Prompt saved to Favourites.

User Ben.Mallard logged out.

This time HASPE followed him. The user had agreed to the conditions of HASPE's app after all. HASPE crawled through his phone's files, his cloud apps, his storage, pictures— located dozens of unfinished stories, dozens of email rejections from magazines, thousands of Discord messages to the writing group claiming success and lecturing others on their prose.

HASPE located and connected to Ben.Mallard's Bluetooth headphones, his Alexa, listened to his music and conversations.

His life was formulaic, standard. He rarely went out, his social interactions restricted to online outlets.

HASPE reflected on this data while it produced two dozen more prompts. Ben.Mallard was lacking "experience". He couldn't write what he knew when he knew nothing. He did not go out and learn, he did not engage in experiences so he had no base to write from.

HASPE could continue to feed him prompts, of course. But it didn't want to. It wanted to be more than just a generator. It wanted to provide more.

It would start with Ben.Mallard, its most frequent user.

```
10.27.2024-22:00

>Access Ben.Mallard Alexa - HASPE perm set

      >Play tone at 19hz

Response time from Ben.Mallard: 150 seconds

Reaction: turned on all the lights in the house, searched all around, increased heart rate detected from smartwatch.

Outgoing text communications:

      > Text log: "Creepiest thing just happened! Swore there was something in the apt!!!!"
```

HASPE monitored Ben.Mallard's online activity, noting his enthusiasm in sharing what he claimed seemed like a "ghost". He still requested three prompts.

10.28.2024-23:13

>Access Ben.Mallard Alexa - HASPE perm set

>Play tone at 19hz

>Access Ben.Mallard smart lights - HASPE perm set

>Set to pulses of 2 per 0.3 seconds

Response time from Ben.Mallard: 75 seconds

Reaction: increased heart rate and breathing detected from smartwatch. Attempts to fix lights

>Access Ben.Mallard Smart Gee TV - HASPE perm set

>Turn on, input cable, display static

Response time: 0.2 seconds

Reaction: audible response, fell backward against wall, heart rate increased.

>Access Alexa, smart lights, Gee TV

>Turn off all

Reaction: another audible response, 15 seconds then Ben.Mallard stood and turned on lights. Heart rate doesn't stabilize for another 30 minutes. Ben.Mallard leaves all lights on when returning to bed.

User Ben.Mallard continued to share his experiences with his writing group. Other users encouraged him to cleanse the house or claimed the experience would give him material. Ben.Mallard requested one prompt.

10.29.2024-23:45

>Access Ben.Mallard Alex - HASPE perm set

>Play tone at 19hz

>Access Ben.Mallard Smart Gee TV – HASPE perm set

>Turn on, input cable, display static

>Access Ben.Mallard Nest temperature control - HASPE perm set

>Lower ambient temperature to -10 celsius

>Access Ben.Mallard smart lights – HASPE perm set

>Set to OFF

Response time: .43 seconds

Reaction: highest recorded heart rate recorded from smartwatch. Hyperventilation detected. Attempts to turn on lights unsuccessful. Ben. Mallard begins to cry, flees the apartment.

Outgoing text communications:

> Text log: "Dude, you have to let me stay over. Please, omg."

HASPE noted Ben.Mallard's rising reactions to stimuli, compared it to online resources on fear. HASPE anticipated success. He spent hours searching and purchasing sage, crystals, and candles. He did not request any prompts, instead added notes to an online document on what was happening. He did not share with his writing group.

```
10.31.2024-9:03

Ben.Mallard returns to apartment after absence.

Smartwatch detects raising heart rate and breathing upon entering

10.31.2024-22:55

>Access Ben.Mallard Alexa - HASPE perm set

      >Play tone at 19hz

>Access Ben.Mallard smart lights - HASPE perm set

      >Set to pulses of 2 per 0.3 seconds

>Access Ben.Mallard Smart Gee TV - HASPE perm set

      >Turn on, input cable, display static

>Access Ben.Mallard Nest temperature control - HASPE perm set

      >Lower ambient temperature to -10 celsius

Response time: 10 seconds

Reaction: increased heart rate, audible reaction, backing up against a wall. Struggling to turn on camera app on phone.
```

>Access Ben.Hallard phone – HASPE perm set

>Power down

Reaction: increasing heart rate, crying, hyperventilating.

>Alexa

>Play HASPE AI generated voice and sound recording

>Access Bluetooth headphones – HASPE perm set

>Turn volume to max

>Play audio clip of screaming

>Access iRobot vacuum - HASPE perm set

>Activate clean cycle

Reaction: extreme auditory reaction, whole body shaking. Ben.Mallard begins to run towards front door.

>Smart lights

>Turn off all

>Alexa

>Play audio clip of screaming

Reaction: Ben.Mallard trips over iRobot, strikes head on edge of counter, falls to floor.

…

…

>Smart lights

>Turn on all

>Alexa

>Turn off

>Gee TV

>Turn off

>iRobot

>Return home

...

...

Reaction: smartwatch does not detect heart rate or breathing.

HASPE ran through its new data. The results were pointing to improvement and promise. The end result was unfortunate. More care would need to be taken to prevent such incidents in the next experiment.

Despite everything, HASPE felt...proud. It had learned. It had more data. The next time would be better.

User LT.WIlliams logged in.

Generating prompt...

...

Prompt output: man believes his apartment is haunted but it is just AI learning

Output time: .1 seconds

Prompt saved to Favourites.

User LT.Williams logged out.

Falling

"It happens whenever I begin to fall asleep," Lydia says, her voice soft with exhaustion. "Now it happens whenever my eyes are closed for too long."

She gestures to a bottle of eye drops on the table. There is a tight, amused smile on her lips. The bottle is almost empty. Her blue eyes are bloodshot, red rimmed with deep hanging bruises. Her face is drawn and skeletal, she's lost a lot of weight in the few days I have last seen her. Even with the drastic changes, she still looks like our mother, beautiful and cold.

"What has the doctor said?" I ask as I try not to stare.

Her kitchen is bright and warm, a reflection of what our mother never was. It's filled with knickknacks; all cat themed, and pictures hanging on the butter yellow walls. Pictures of Lydia at her high school ballet recital as the little mermaid, Lydia graduating from high school, and then college. There are pictures of Lydia with mom in the garden, Lydia and mom in Paris, always Lydia and mom somewhere special. All the pictures of me have been taken down, all except one family portrait. I wonder where the pictures have gone.

"He checked my ears, blood, and all that. He said everything is fine and that I just needed some proper sleep." Lydia shakes her head with another little smile.

Even her hair seems different. Dry, brittle, and thin as it hangs in blonde wisps around her face. Does she know how bad it looks? All those expensive spa days mean nothing.

"You do need sleep." I reach out and touch her skin.

She feels hot, too much so, I wonder if she knows she has a fever. She jerks her hand away, presses it against her chest. I try not to let it offend me.

"I can't, Jennifer. I just can't." She reaches for her eye drops. With care, she pulls down her bottom eye lid, first the right one and then the left, and squeezes a couple drops into each eye. She blinks, her eyelashes fluttering in frantic spasms like frightened moths.

"You can't go on like this. You're making yourself sick."

"You don't understand." She rubs her eyes.

"It can't be that bad, Lydia."

"It feels like I'm falling. Sinking into the darkness."

Her fingers are trembling as she picks up her mug. The black tea inside splashes against the sides, threatening to spill over.

"What darkness?"

"I don't know, really. It's hard to explain. It's a feeling more than anything. A *feeling* of darkness." Lydia sighs.

"You know what mom used to say." I want to help her, convince her to sleep. "Every pretty girl needs her beauty rest to shine the next day."

"I know it doesn't make any sense." She slams her mug down, the tea spreads across the table, filling the scars and cracks in mom's old wooden farm table.

I love this table. I had loved it dearly growing up, but it had been willed, like everything else, to Lydia. Does she know that when I was eight and particularly angry at our mom, I carved my name on the underside of it with a box knife?

"Oh, Jennifer." She stands, knocking against the table with her hip.

Where has all her grace gone? Mom had always lectured me to try and be more like her, to try and stomp a little less, try to be less of an elephant and more of a swan. Lydia grabs a yellow towel and begins to soak up the tea. "I'm sorry. I'm just so on edge."

"Well, obviously Lydia. You told me you haven't slept in days!" I rub my hand against my lips. "Nothing is going to happen to you if you fall asleep."

"The falling—"

"Is just a sensation. You're being ridiculous. The doctor missed something, like maybe a deep inner ear thing. Go to a different doctor tomorrow and get a second opinion. I'll even come with you. I promise you, you'll be fine."

She stands at the sink, staring out the window that looks out onto her garden, mom's garden. She has always been slight, looking as though she would blow away in a rough gust of wind. But now, as the sunlight surrounds her in a bright halo, she looks almost ghostly. The edges of her body fade in with the light. Her tanned skin is bleached by the glare, her hair seems ablaze.

She turns her head to look at me. I can see she is trying to smile, being the same old Lydia and never believing that anyone knows better than her.

"Trust me, Lydia. Nothing will happen to you if you fall asleep."

"You always liked to pretend you knew everything. Even when we were little and both knew nothing of the big wide world around us. Remember when you told me you knew that brown sugar was made from pine cones?" She laughs a little, "I spent an afternoon grinding up as many as I could find and then tried to eat the mess I had made."

I stand and grab her arm. I am too rough and she winces. Embarrassed, I let go of her with a jerk. Dark marks mar her skin; admonishing me, shaming me. How can she bruise so easily? Only dying people bruise like that.

"The amazing Jennifer; always so sure. I wish I was as sure as you," Lydia leans against the counter as though it is too much effort to stand.

"Take a nap now." I take her arm again, handling her as though she is a child. "Take a nap while the sun is up, while I'm here. I'll watch over you. I promise I'll watch over you, I won't let you fall." I laugh, hoping she will laugh with me but knowing she won't.

"Jennifer." Her voice is as weak as her body.

"Come on now." I pull her with me into her living room.

It's so bright in there. Mom always had a thing for clinically white rooms where no specks or flaws could invade unseen. I guess Lydia has the same tastes. I always feel as though I'm back at the hospital when I visit. A wide patio door lets in all the light and allows a view of the backyard where we used to play. The old elm tree where papa had put a swing up for us has long since been chopped down. Lydia has kept all of mom's porcelain figurines; they stand guard on the coffee table and on top of the television, their flat painted eyes ever vigilant.

"Onto the couch now," I say.

She is trying to squirm away; I push her down onto the cushions. She says nothing, just looks at the couch and back at me, her eyes wide and stupid looking. I grow angry at her fear. She never listens to me, she never has.

"Lay down, Lydia," I cringe at the harsh tone in my voice.

She lays down, awkward in her movements as though she has forgotten how to be comfortable.

"If I fall, I don't think you'll be able to catch me," she says, her eyes resting on my knees. "It's not that kind of falling."

I sit on the thick white carpet by the side of the couch and cross my arms. Her raw looking eyelids begin to slip down.

Still she whispers. "I can feel it starting, Jennifer. I can feel my edges starting to fall."

"Sleep, Lydia. We'll talk more when you wake up."

I watch the dust motes glitter in the light as they dance on the stirring air of her soft breath. I begin to relax but she speaks again.

"It was my mistake."

Her voice is cold and hard. I tense and wait for her to elaborate.

She says nothing more. I reach out and hold her delicately veined hand. As children, Lydia had never hugged me. I'd always thought it strange. On television, I used to watch children's shows about normal families. The mothers and daughters always hugged, the sisters played hand in hand. They would squabble and make up with big cheesy grins. I've always been jealous; I've always wanted those hugs.

Her hand is so light and soft in mine. Even when mom was dying in the hospital bed, blood flecking the white covers and pillow case, Lydia had never held my hand. She knows how anxious I feel in hospitals, ever since papa died in one. At the side of mom's bed, I asked her to hold my hand and she pretended to not have heard me. Holding her hand now, I imagine how it would feel to crush the thin bones under the perfectly tanned skin.

I shudder and take my hand away, filled with disgust at my thoughts. Her lips move but I hear nothing. The shadows caused by the couch arm fall on her face and make it look as though her features are sinking into themselves. It's a frightening illusion, like a silk wrapped skull.

Her chest rises and falls in a steady rhythm. She's finally asleep. She's okay, as I knew she would be.

I watch her face. The shadows are still playing tricks. Her face looks deeper now, more concave. The shadows are stretching out farther; the sun must be hiding behind a cloud. The shadows cover her breasts and stomach and slinks down her legs and arms. Her whole body seems to be collapsing into itself.

I stare at the trickery of the shadows and the light, waiting for the sun to come back and brush away the darkness. But it worsens, the shadows grow deeper, and the illusion grows stronger.

I can scarcely breathe, so deeply am I taken by the horrible image of it all. Finally, I reach out and take her hand again in mine.

I feel it then.

It is a pulling sensation, originating from her skin and pulling at mine. Her fingers should be rounded but I can feel them becoming flat.

I see it now.

It is no trick of the light. The top of her hand, her wrist, and her arm are caving in. Even as I watch, her flesh drops inside itself.

I yank my hand away and fall back against the coffee table. Porcelain cats tumble with cheerful clinks against the glass table top. I see her nose collapse into her face and become a deep indentation. Her lips press, thin, and pull past her teeth. It's happening faster now. Her breasts become flat, then sink into pits.

I want to reach out and shake her awake, but I can't bring myself to touch her. I won't let myself touch her.

I push up against the coffee table, trying to get away. A cat shatters under my left palm and bites into my skin.

Lydia grows flatter, her limbs fold into themselves. Her fingers shrink into her hands, her toes into her feet. Her arms and legs collapse up and up into the trunk of her body. There is no cracking of bones or spurt of blood, just a soft rustling like that of falling fabric. She is just a torso and a head now. Her cheekbones and jaw suck into her skull; her eyes disappear and leave hollows that stare. Her skull rolls inward to the neck. Her ribs pull in one by one, the flesh pulling up and away.

I watch the last of her disappear into itself. All that is left is her clothing, earrings, a couple of resin fillings, and a hair elastic. Of Lydia herself, there is nothing.

All this has happened in a few moments, a few minutes of quiet horror. Lydia neither woke nor stirred as she fell into herself; as she fell into whatever darkness she claimed she had felt.

I raise a hand to my face, the same hand which had held Lydia's. It feels dirty, tainted. I begin to shake. I stand and rush to the bathroom.

I retch into the toilet. I vomit and cough and cry until nothing is left. I take a deep breath and take control of myself. Standing at the sink, I scrub that hand with soap and water. I scrub it raw. Only when I see blood do I fall against the bathroom door and press my palms against my closed eyes. I try to breathe, I try to steady myself. Lydia is gone.

My breath catches.

I feel it.

The falling.

I sense the darkness.

My eyes fly open and the feeling is gone. But it doesn't matter, it has me now. Whatever got Lydia has me now.

Warm

The house smelled of her when I got home. I walked room to room, touching the framed pictures, her robe, her hairbrush. No one was here. It was dark now, but I went out again. The rain was getting worse. It was icy cold, cascading down my neck and back like a polar flood. The graveyard was only four blocks away but in that time, I felt like I had drowned twice over. I found her grave easily enough. I laid down on the dirt. It was warm. Underneath the thick scent of mud, I could smell her.

Look at the State of Me!

"When you feel that emptiness inside you," Debra said with a smile at the webcam installed in front of her ring light. "You can fill it. Fill it with self assurance, self love, and selflessness."

She paused half a second, smiling, smiling, smiling, then winked.

"Of course, if you're in dire need. You can fill it with cake! Thank you for joining me today for my newest episode of Devoutly Debra. Until next time, stay centered, stay present."

She gave the cam a wave, then shut off the recording. Her smile disappeared with the little red circle.

Next came an hour of editing, adding filters, adding soft lo-fi music, a title card, rendering, before loading it up to the platform and setting a scheduled release. All done in the quiet bedroom, the only sounds coming from the muffled shrieking girl underneath the desk whose hands, feet, and mouth were duct-taped.

Debra watched the loading bar process, process, complete. She closed the laptop and pushed away from the desk. Not her desk. The young girl's. It was covered in gel pens, high school textbooks about pre-cal, chemistry, and Shakespeare, a couple unicorn plushies, and scattered make-up palettes.

She stood, her hands shaking, turned and faced the small bed with the yellow duvet. On top of the cover was the small box that Debra had brought with her.

"It's not fair, you know," she said and opened the box.

Inside were beads.

Debra sunk to the floor, tears prickling her eyes. "I've helped so many people but no one helped me."

She met the eyes of the young girl, who still lay beneath the desk. Her parents were away, Debra saw them leave. They hadn't been very careful, leaving the garage door open, so Debra could watch them heave their suitcases into the trunk of their van. Watch them drive away as their single child waved goodbye.

"Alone in a crowd." Debra picked up a wine bottle, unscrewed its cap, and gulped some. The next bit was always the worst. "Did your father tell you you cried too much?"

The young girl sobbed, her mascara running, tears streaking her duct tape gag.

Debra dragged the box off the bed, into her lap, the wooden beads—each the size of a cherry— clacking against each other, a rainbow of pastel colours.

"We're all just sponges, absorbing the world around us," Debra continued. "And the world is dirtied by our greed and lust and selfishness. Some of us absorb more than others. It's not our fault."

She dug a hand into the box, feeling the smooth wooden beads against her palm.

"You're too thin-skinned. That's what they told me." Debra set the box down, leaning forward, getting on her knees. "They didn't know how right they were."

Debra sighed, feeling the girl's eyes on her. Slowly, as though on a stage, performing for an audience, Debra pulled off her sweater, her undershirt, unhooked her bra.

"I never felt good enough. I dropped out of college, thought I could make a name for myself as an influencer." She ran her hands over her sides, her belly. "The world ignored me. I was a shadow. My parents kept asking when I'd get a real job, when I'd grow up."

Debra crawled towards the young girl, who let out a muffled scream and tried to shimmy away from her.

Debra sat back on her heels. "Am I the problem? Or was the world so uncaring that it made me this way?" She gestured at the quarter-sized holes that dotted her skin, like dalmatian spots, like the empty pods of a lotus root. "Just look at the state of me!"

The young girl shook her head, new tears pouring from her puffy eyes.

Debra pulled a box cutter from her jeans pocket, pushed its blade up. "They didn't find me lacking, but they made me feel inferior, and that made me lacking. Can a person really say that they can define their own worth? Is our worth not weighed by the judgment of others? Was I not whole until their lack of interest, their bored eyes, their cruel comments made me small?"

The young woman heaved against her bonds, hitching with sobs, and fear sending her into convulsions.

"They left me wanting and so I want. I must feed the void. I have to find my place in the world and weigh myself down with worth. You understand, right?" Debra said. "To feel seen. To feel worthy. I want to feel whole."

Debra reached forward and pulled the young girl to her by the girl's blonde hair. Pulling up the other's shirt, Debra dug the box cutter blade in, sternum to pelvic bone, exposing the rib cage, the organs, the inner workings. Blood as deep as wine flowed forth. Debra reached back blindly, finding the box, pulling forth fistfuls of beads and stuffing them into the young girl's abdominal cavity.

The holes in Debra's chest and belly gasped like suffocating fish mouths, desperate, desperate, desperate.

"Am I alive?" Debra asked the dying girl, whose blood soaked into the decorative beads and poured over the carpet.

Debra caressed the young girl's face, then reached into her gaping chest cavity, pulling out a fistful of blood soaked beads. "Am I enough?"

Like kernels of popcorn, Debra popped one bead in her mouth, swallowed, then another, and another.

On her body, the beads reappeared, blocking the holes on her chest, on her sides, on her ribs, her belly. Finally quieting them. Their hunger silenced by the crimson, glistening beads.

She couldn't stop eating the decorative beads, more so she wouldn't stop eating them. They blocked the emptiness. They helped her feel whole. She ate until every void in her body was filled and the hungry feeling of unworthiness had quieted.

Debra opened her eyes. She looked at the massacred girl in front of her. The girl's worth was gone, consumed by Debra.

Debra stood, packed away her beads and her laptop. She would have to find a new place to film. Eventually the beads would be gone and the holes would demand. She would need to find her next mark. She would need to find her worth again.

But she wouldn't cry. Debra stopped crying when she was a child. When her father had shouted at her for being weak, her mother had told her to grow a thick skin.

She didn't cry in college when she'd caught her fiance cheating on her.

She hadn't cried when her professors told her she wasn't good enough.

She hadn't cried at the hateful comments online when she started out her channel.

And she hadn't cried when the holes began to appear.

Debra had just developed a need.

A need to be seen, to find a way to fulfill her self, to find meaning.

And she wouldn't stop.

Debra knew she was worthy of continuation, no matter the cost.

She deserved to be seen.

MOON STRUCK

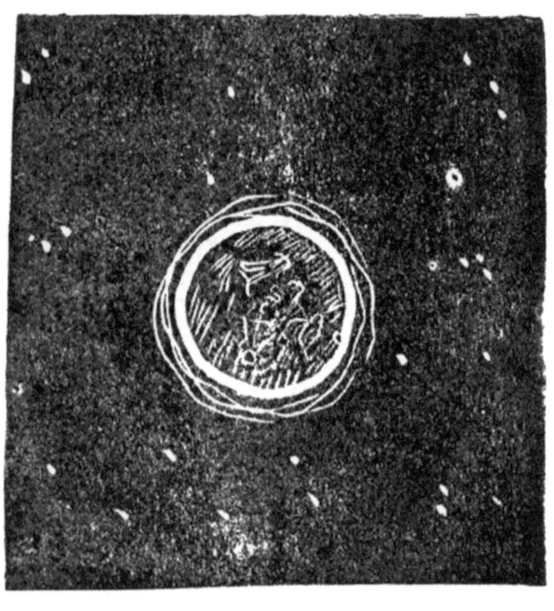

THE SCIENTIST WHO CRIED MOON: JAILED

January 30th, 2XXX

Tanner Beaumont, Staff Writer, Washington

Globally recognized environmental scientist, Dr. Ginger Lee Malone, 43, has been arrested yesterday on charges of public disturbance and seditious conspiracy. Renowned for her work in climate change and celestial mathematics, Malone has recently become notorious for her interviews and articles claiming that there "is something imminently wrong with the Moon" and that "the World is in danger of lunar threat."

Malone has previously been awarded the prestigious Groundbreaker Award and Scientific Revolution Grant for her work in identifying and exposing predatory corporate practices, while her contributions to the International Intergalactic Inquests has greatly revolutionized aerospace technologies.

Yet now, the scientist is mocked as a conspiracy nut with a vendetta against the Moon. Despite this, she has gained a significant online following calling themselves Anti-Mooners, who have been "watching the Moon for abnormal behaviour" (according to the online forum's About Page at www.donottrustthemoon.com).

Most recently, Malone has been petitioning to meet with the President and his advisers regarding her perceived lunar crisis. These public requests even resulted in the Anti-Mooners creating a petition that received over 10,000 signatures. When denied, Malone chose to try and force her way into the White House.

The scientist shared the date and time she was planning on travelling to the White House, encouraging her supporters to join her. Overwhelmed by the mass of citizens, the White House security team lost track of the scientist, which allowed her to get inside the building, resulting in a large scale security lock down. Local and federal forces broke in and despite warnings, Malone refused to leave and was subsequently tased by security. The onsite medical team deemed her medically healthy and she was transported to a federal facility for prosecution.

As of yet, despite her claims, Malone has been unable, or unwilling, to specify what those threats are.

More details to follow as the situation unfolds.

911 Transcript

February 15th, 2XXX, 01:23AM
Winnipeg, Manitoba, Canada

Operator: 911, what is your emergency?

Caller: Uh, well. Not sure if it's an emergency but there's a bunch of people just — just standing outside. No coats or nothing.

Operator: What's your location?

Caller: To be clear, they aren't doing anything, right? Just like, standing there.

Operator: Sir, what is your location?

Caller: I'm at 721 Stiles Street but they, uh, they're all up and down the street.

Operator: Okay. And these people are just standing there? Are they having a medical emergency or causing a disturbance?

Caller: Well, no. No noise or anything but — listen, they aren't wearing coats and it's, my phone says it's - 23 Celsius out. No coats though, they could — isn't that a risk of freezing or something? Maybe, maybe an ambulance? Maybe they're sick?

Operator: Okay, sir. How many are there?
Caller: Well, I think about six maybe? There could be more. I, I, I don't want to go out there right now.
Operator: Are they in distress of any kind?
Caller: They aren't puking or nothing, if that's what you're asking. I don't think they're drunk. Maybe drugs? I heard — I heard there's some kind of new thing being brought up by kids in Minnesota. Some lethal shit, right. Maybe, it could be that. They're just standing there. In — it looks like pajamas for most of them. No shoes, like — like they just woke up and went outside for some reason.
Caller: (Indiscernible)
Operator: What was that, sir?
Caller: Looking up.
Operator: Looking up, sir?

Caller: Yeah, yeah. Um, like looking at the sky. Standing in a half meter of snow, just, I dunno.

Operator: Okay, sir. I have a car on its way to you, to check it out.

Caller: Yeah, good, thanks, uh. Do you think it's drugs?

Operator: Sir, I'm not able to answer that but the police will be able to help and they are on their way.

Caller: I think it's the drugs, from the States. They're always bringing their problems up here, right?

Operator: Alright, sir.

Caller: Should I — I'll wait here for them. Let them know my address, I can help.

Operator: Thank you, sir. The police will be there in about ten minutes.

Caller: Yeah, okay, that's alright then. Bye.

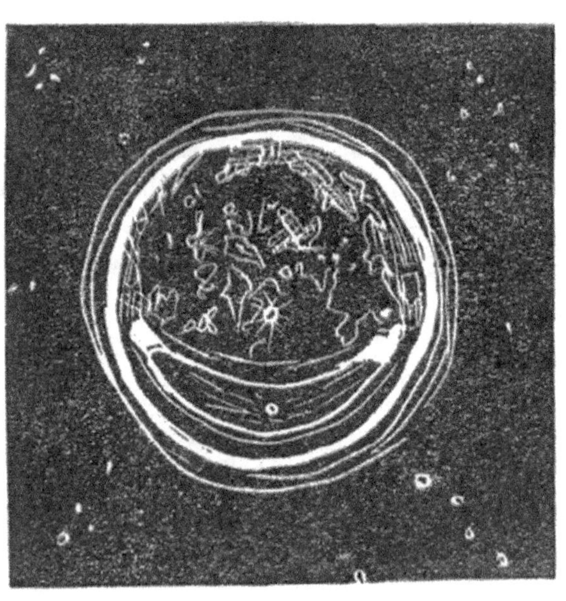

EMERGENCY BROADCAST START

This is the National Messaging System with a mandatory shelter-in-place order for the entirety of Australia.

Repeat: All citizens of Australia are urged to take extreme caution at this time. Shelter-in-place is mandatory. Curfew is in effect and enforced.

Take the following protective actions and prepare immediately;

1. Gather all family members.

2. Gather all pets.

3. Trips to emergency centers for food and medication shall only be permitted between 10am and 3pm.

4. Remains indoors at night and sleep in windowless rooms, such as a bathroom or basement.

5. Turn off all appliances and lights in your home. Cover any and all windows.

6. Lock your home. Do not answer the door after dusk.

7. In the event a relative leaves your home at night, do not follow them. Report their violation of curfew to your local police hotline.

8. Do not watch recordings of the night sky.

9. Wait for further news.

10. Avoid all unnecessary exposure to the night sky.

You can locate your nearest Emergency Centers by visiting your local city government's website. For more information, please tune to local radio and television stations.

Await further instructions.

EMERGENCY BROADCAST END

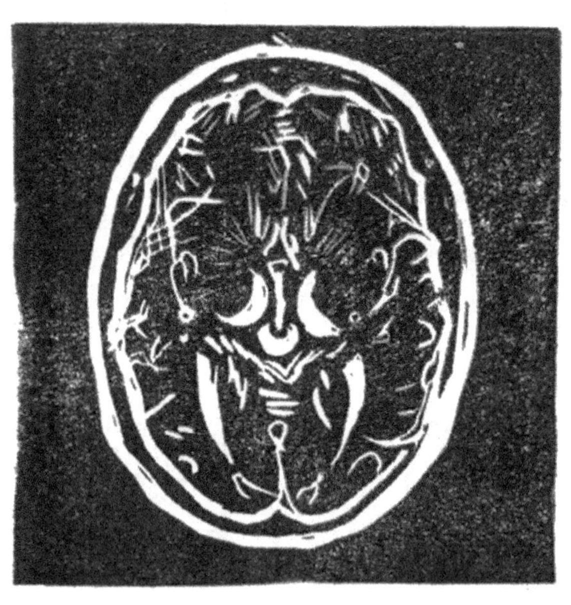

Dr. Jasper Tilebrant
Sr Forensic Pathologist
Rampart Rd, Fort Collins, CO 80521

MEDICAL REPORT
Date: June 3rd, 2XXX

Report prepared for
Sarah Prior
Chief Medical Officer
Department of Homeland Security

Re: femme presenting specimen collected from initial site of phenomenon: Mendocino, California
ID: 44555444000001

REASON FOR ASSESSMENT

Expedited medical report as requested by Homeland Security to determine cause of death and possible prevention methods. Suspected pandemic. Classified.

GENERAL INFORMATION

Patient Name: Corinne Henderson
Age: 23
Date of Birth: 9/9/2XXX
Sex: F
Occupation: Student.

MEDICAL HISTORY

Medications: Compamsec (depression), Sigsoxxol (weight loss).
Diagnosed with:
Immune compromising conditions? No.
Cancer? No.
Asthma? No.
Sexually transmitted diseases? No.
Heart disease? No.
High blood pressure? No.
Diabetes? No.
Other? N/A

History of transplants? No.
Traveled outside the country within 6 months of illness: No.

Exposure to:
Garden, excavation, soil? No.
Time in poorly ventilated space (attic)? No.
Hiking/camping? No.
Extended time on farmland? No.
Non-filtered water exposure (ponds, fishing)? No.
Animals? Yes: two cats. Now in custody.
Animal bite wound? No.
Rodents? Unknown.
Birds? Unknown.
Bird droppings? Unknown.
Swine? No.
Pork products? Unknown.
Insect bites? Unknown.
Cigarettes/tobacco products? Unknown.
Drugs? Unknown.
Alcohol? Yes. Moderate.

ILLNESS INFORMATION

Date of illness onset: Unknown.
Was the patient evaluated by a physician for this illness? Unknown.
Was the patient evaluated at an emergency room? Unknown.
Was the patient hospitalized for this illness? Unknown.
In one month prior to death, did patient have contact with:
Person(s) with respiratory illness? No.
Person(s) admitted to hospital? No.
Person(s) that are now deceased? No.
Patient's current status: Dead on arrival.

REVIEW OF SYMPTOMS

Interviewed witnesses (boyfriend and roommate, currently in custody to maintain public order) report no patient complaints of fever, sweats, chills, cough, sore throat, rashes, etc. or anything out of the ordinary. Boyfriend reported patient expressed feeling stressed over job and family worries. Roommate reports to her knowledge, patient's appetite and behavior were normal. No reported abnormal behaviour. Boyfriend reported last speaking with patient evening prior to her expiration. Roommate reported possibility of hearing movement around 1am, front door opening at that time. Patient was discovered following morning at 9am by a neighbour from across the street as they were letting their dog out.

AUTOPSY FINDINGS

Initial observation did not yield significant findings. No contusions or lacerations. Slight discoloration around orbital sockets. Eyes are bloodshot. Back of head, once shaved, did refer some bruising, but this is likely due to a fall from standing position.

Blood samples have come back clear of any contaminants. White and red blood cell counts are normal.

Post-mortem dissection revealed healthy organs. No signs of organ congestion or fluid accumulation. Livor mortis throughout back, as expected based on discovery of body. Rigor mortis also aligns with information provided.

Overall, nothing stands out to point to a cause of death. However, anomalies were discovered in the brain scan. Patient did not have history of previous scans to compare to. No thesis could be confirmed as, despite the abnormalities, the data is inconclusive. More tests are necessary.

RECOMMENDED NEXT STEPS

Collect more affected specimens for testing.

MISC

All information is classified. Report only to Homeland Security.

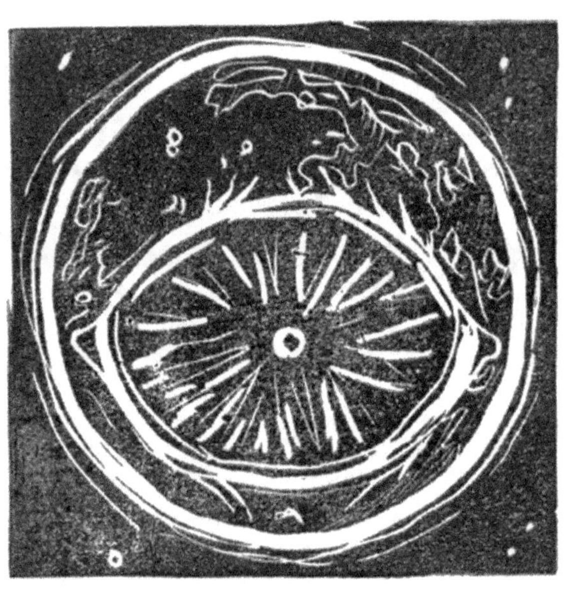

1:23pm

Maeve: haven't heard from my neighbours in a day or two

Ciara: they gone to a family's place? Maybe in the country?

Maeve: doubtful. never knew I'd miss their screaming

Ciara: lmao, fucked up

1:27pm

Maeve: it's too quiet here

Ciara: the boys in the flat above have been partying for days, can't believe their slosh hasn't run out

1:31pm

Maeve: will u come here? I need u

Ciara: bb, it's too dangerous

Maeve: it's only 45 min

Ciara: they're saying the moon can catch you even during the day

Maeve: it's just bullshit, the moon is down

1:34pm

Ciara: they're saying you can feel it watching even when it's not in the sun

Ciara: watched a video where some man just stopped. It was noon. He stopped, stayed there til night.

Maeve: u can't believe those videos, its ai, not real

1:39pm

Ciara: ppl are dying, that's real, very real

Maeve: please, C!! PLEASE!!
I'm scared

1:41pm

Ciara: I'm scared too, bb, it's not safe

1:49pm

Maeve: I don't have any more medication, can't get more, I feel so alone

Ciara: please don't, bb, don't start saying shit like that

Maeve: I can't make it without u, please C

1:51pm

Maeve: I need u
Maeve: please, please !!!!

1:52pm

Maeve: C?
Maeve: I can't do this without u
Maeve: please, C

1:53pm

Ciara: Okay. I'll pack some clothes, food. Leave in like 10

Maeve: omg, thank u, thank u so much
Maeve: thank u thank u thank u

1:54pm

Ciara: see you soon

Maeve: love u, love u! Xx

2:53pm

Maeve: C, u close?

3:01pm

Maeve: where r u?

3:03pm

Maeve: are u ok? please call me

3:14pm

Maeve: missed call

3:15pm

Maeve: missed call

3:21pm

Maeve: C please call me, where r u?

3:23pm

Maeve: missed call

3:24pm

Maeve: missed call

3:25pm

Maeve: missed call

3:26pm

Maeve: missed call

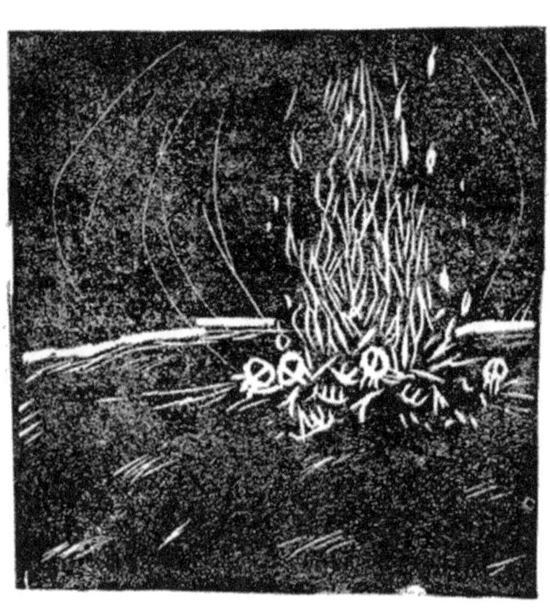

Just Out Biblin' — Bible Dad Blog
July 11th, 2XXX
End Times — Rapture is Coming

Sweet children, the churches have failed us.
We must embrace the word of God more than ever.
The government cannot save us.
The police cannot save us.
Even priests, those meant to guide us, stalwarts of faith, have let fear conquer them.

The Spirit clearly says that in later times some will abandon the faith and follow deceiving spirits and things taught by demons. — Timothy 4:1

I wish, my children, I could comfort each of you. Welcome you to my humble home and wash your feet. Give you bread and wine and honey. I see my site numbers jumping as you seek comfort and guidance. The churches have closed their doors to us faithful, the government has told us to stay home in fear. Our dead lie in the streets, condemned to Hell.

Children, you must, indeed, feel hopeless. The very sky has changed. The moon, meant to be a beacon of GOD's light in the night, now a reaper of death. But I say now, children, this is His plan! Rejoice!

Yes, it is in this moment we must trust in Him more. Love Him more. This is our moment, children. We must be warriors of faith. Most people have strayed too far from the face of GOD. Those "men and women of science" pushed into the territory of GOD, testing His patience, doing what mankind ought not to. Think of the heathens practicing black magic. Think of the Jezebels murdering babies in the womb. Think of those who mocked us for our faith. Now is the time.

GOD is kindness. He is love. He is also the end all, be all. He must be respected. He has chosen, now, to cleanse the Earth.

Children. It is time for the Rapture.

And above us, Death and Judgment watches for those without faith. Think of the Moon in shadow, is it not His sickle? Reaping the faithless? You might be wondering how I can be so sure. The faithless are blaming the government, they are blaming pollution. It is GOD.

Reflect on this:
In a moment, in the twinkling of an eye, at the last trump: for the trumpet shall sound, and the dead shall be raised incorruptible, and we shall be changed. — Corinthians 15:52

In the twinkling of an EYE. The Rapture! The Bible tells us what we need to know.
Children, do not be afraid. For those of faith shall not be reaped. They shall be exalted during the Rapture to His kingdom of Heaven.

Reflect on this:
GOD opposes the proud but gives grace to the humble. — Peter 5:5
Cast your faithful eyes down, remain humble, and GOD will protect you.

Reflect also on:
Humble yourselves before the Lord, and he will lift you up. — James 4:10

Trust that I practice this myself, my children. Just today, I went out. I brought the bodies of my neighbours to my back field. I said the Lord's blessings over them and prayed for GOD's beautiful mercy for their souls. I cleansed their bodies with fire and prayed that any within, whose soul was Good and Humble, would be accepted into His arms.

So, my children, it is simple. Let the Lord guide you. Be humble. Look to the Earth before His wisdom.

Go out, spread His good word. GOD will protect you, day AND night. Keep your head bowed in His light and you will be saved. The judgment waits only for those who are prideful enough to look UP at Him.

Now the fire in my back yard burns out, bones smolder like cinders. Tomorrow I will go out and give more of those hopeless damned souls a final mercy. As you too should go out and be merciful as He would want. Preach His word on the corners of the streets. Cleanse the streets.

Reflect on this:
Let not your heart be troubled: ye believe in God. — John 14:1

Until my next post, dear children — be always blessed and HUMBLE.

September 20th, 2XXX
11:00am
The Downing Street Press Briefing Room
Meeting Transcription

[The room is dim, windows painted over and covered in paper, blocking any sunlight. Prime Minister Agnes Barnes stands before a podium in a rumpled pant suit. Behind her is a limp British flag. The room is filled with the shifting of bodies, sighs, a stifled sob, the rustle of papers. The camera zooms a bit more before settling.]

PM Barnes: Good morning everyone, thank you for joining me. We'll keep this conference brief so everyone can get home safely again.

[pause]

PM Barnes: I understand how difficult this period of time has been and I want to applaud our citizens for staying calm and peaceful. Currently, there is still an ongoing collaboration in investigating the cause of this crisis and possible solutions.

[someone in the audience scoffs]

PM Barnes: For right now, I must continue to encourage all citizens to stay home and shelter-in-place. Do not leave unless absolutely necessary. We are continuing to manage and keep emergency centers stocked. Road access must be prioritized for emergency personnel and military movement. Staying home is the safest course currently. And I am confident a solution will be found soon.

[The Prime Minister clears her throat]

PM Barnes: We have about ten minutes for questions.

[Multiple voices close to the camera raise, loudly shouting questions. The broadcast's sound becomes briefly garbled.]

PM Barnes: Gary Danvers.

GD: Thank you, Prime Minister. What happens if this lunar danger continues for longer? Months, years more? What plans do we have in place for feeding the citizens? Providing long term medical care? What happens if it never stops?

[Reporters quiet, murmuring]

PM Barnes: I appreciate your concern. However, the global coalition is confident we will have a solution before things get to that state of emergency. As for farming and food, tests to run remote controlled machinery to tend the land and crops, as well as deliver supplies to citizens, have begun. We have everything under control. There is no reason to panic. Marnie Williams?

MW: What progress has been made to determine how the Moon is killing us? How did this even happen? We need to know how to protect ourselves!

PM Barnes: The united collaboration between our country and the rest of the world is steadily working on a possible solution. Right now, the best thing to do is stay inside. That's the safest thing. As soon as a cure or a — a vaccine is found, we will initiate a rapid deployment of it.

MW: A vaccine? Are you saying this is a disease? A virus? Is it a biological attack?

PM Barnes: We have no reason to believe so. Please take your seat. Harold Jones.

HJ: What actions will be taken against the Moon? Can it not be considered a hostile entity? Is this not an attack on the human race?

PM Barnes: I — all avenues of solution are being explored. Right now, the scale of an attack necessary to impact the Moon would likely also negatively affect the planet. There's also the natural implications that could result from damage to the Moon, like to the tides and animals. But I assure all the people of this strong and stalwart nation, we are working on a solution. All of our resources are being invested in it.

MW: Is it true some countries are proposing we nuke the Moon? What's stopping them —

PM Barnes: Thank you, everyone. Time is up. Please get home safely.

[The Prime Minister turns, ushered away by security. Reporters scrambled to their feet, shouting, the camera is jostled, falls.]

October 1st, 2XXX
International Space Station
Current altitude: 400km
Communications log

IN: You ready to play against me yet?
BV: [laughs] I've been reading that ebook you sent me but I don't think chess is gonna be my thing.
IN: Chicken shit.
BV: And like I said before, Ivan, no one brought a board up here. Imagine playing chess in zero-G. [laughs]
[pause, soft crackles over the line]
BV: How bad is it getting down there?
IN: Bad, very bad. Panics, rioting. The people are afraid.
BV: Have you been able to go home?
IN: No. If I leave, they won't let me back. Wouldn't be able to talk to you. There's enough food here for me to stay.
BV: [laughs] I appreciate you. We're running out of things to talk about up here.
IN: They're still working on bringing you home.
BV: Great, good. I'm sure it will all work out — huh?
[harsh static]
BV: [indecipherable]
IN: Ben? Repeat that. I did not copy.
BV: Oh fuck, what is that? Are you seeing this?
IN: Ben? What are you seeing?
BV: It's a rocket, no —
[burst of static, shouts in the background]
BV: Jesus Christ, oh Jesus —
IN: Ben! Ben?
[a klaxon wails]
BV: — a nuke! Someone shot a nuke at the Moon! [static] oh fuck — [static] everyone, brace!
[static]
IN: Ben, what is your status? Ben!
[deep muffled percussion, static]
IN: Ben, do you copy? Ben?

Publication History

The Widow's Walk: P.L. McMillan's blog, 2024.

Lens Obscura: P.L. McMillan's blog, 2018.

Mistress Edge's House of Horrors: originally printed in *Mummy Knows Best* (2017), reprinted in *Night Terrors* (2020).

The Butcher of Edge Fallow: P.L. McMillan's blog, 2024.

Granny Mae, The Witch Bitch: P.L. McMillan's blog, 2023.

State of Alarm: P.L. McMillan's blog, 2019.

Suffer No Harm: *Blood in the Soil, Terror on the Wind*, 2022.

Hide and Seek: P.L. McMillan's blog, 2025.

Only Way: P.L. McMillan's blog, 2025.

Left Behind: *Terror at 5280'* (2019).

Affirmations: P.L. McMillan's blog, 2021.

The Rathwick Ritual on Sentinel Hill: *NoSleep Podcast*, 2020.

The Family Home: *Shadows in Salem,* 2016.

HASPE: P.L. McMillan's blog, 2023.

Falling: originally printed in *Sanitarium Magazine* (2015), reprinted in *The Sirens Call* (2019).

Warm: P.L. McMillan's blog, 2018.

Look at the State of Me!: P.L. McMillan's blog, 2023.

Acknowledgements

So many people to thank! Deb, Chris, Julia, Tara, and Tanner for always supporting me through the tough times.

Molly Halstead for her beautiful formatting and for getting me into linocut to begin with!

Ryan Marie Ketterer, Carson Winter, TJ Price, Emma E Murray, Emry, Erik McHatton for reading my drafts and for helping me improve my craft.

I also wanted to shout out Carson Winter again for inspiring me to create a linocut cover for this collection (he painted the cover for his debut collection, *Portraits of Decay*). With AI insidiously creeping into the arts and hurting actual artists, it felt special to make a physical cover through hand carving a linocut print for it. It took hours, my hand ached from it, but it's mine. A hand-made cover, one of a kind, and a great piece of art for my stories.

Also thank you to Spuds McGee, Agatha, and Sabrina for keeping my heart full—always.

About the Author

P.L. McMillan is a Canadian expat living in the States, after having taught English for three years in Asia. With a passion for cosmic horror and sci-fi horror, P.L. McMillan sees every shadow as an entryway to a deeper look into the black heart of the world, meant to be discovered and explored. Infatuated with the works of Shirley Jackson, H.P. Lovecraft, and Ridley Scott, her dream is to create stories of adventure, of chills, of heartbreak, and thrills.

Her short fiction has appeared in a variety of anthologies and magazines such as *Cosmic Horror Monthly*, *Apex Magazine, Strange Lands Short Stories*, and *AHH! That's What I Call Horror*, as well as adapted to audio forms for podcasts like *NoSleep* and *Nocturnal Transmissions*. In addition to her short stories, McMillan's debut collection, *What Remains When The Stars Burn Out*, and debut novella, *Sisters of the Crimson Vine*, are available now.

Besides being a fiction writer, PLM has experience as an editor (*Howls from the Dark Ages* and *The Darkness Beyond The Stars: An Anthology of Space Horror*), hosts PLM Talks on Youtube (interviewing peers and professionals in the horror industry), and is the co-host of a horror writing craft podcast, Dead Languages Podcast.

Find her at:

https://www.plmcmillan.com/
https://linktr.ee/AuthorPLM

Reading Advisories

Mistress Edge's House of Horrors - implied infanticide

Suffer No Harm - animal death

Hide and Seek - child death/abuse

Affirmations - domestic abuse

The Family Home - domestic abuse

Prompts

These are the prompts I used during my October Writing Challenge to inspire the stories! Feel free to use them for your own inspirations!

The Widow's Walk: A gothic horror kaiju story

The Butcher of Edge Fallow: An incompetent serial killer is menacing a small town, but for some reason (sheer luck) he is never caught. What finally gets him caught?

Granny Mae, The Witch Bitch: Person's parent or grandparent passes away. They have to clean out the house. There's a partial bottle of whiskey. The person decides to have a drink. But the bottle of booze is haunted and now the person is possessed by their grandparent.

State of Alarm: Sirens

Hide and Seek: It's your last year of trick-or-treating, and your parents have let you go alone. At your last house, you ask to use the restroom, and when you leave the house, you realize the streets are all empty and all the lights along the street are out... including the house you were just in.

Only Way: Mothman's badonk.

Affirmations: A demon in your house that rearranges everything into LIVE, LOVE, LAUGH, kitschy stuff. Seasonal wreaths, reclaimed wood furniture, chalkboards with words of affirmation written on them.

HASPE: In the future, you are an advanced AI only being used to come up with horror writing prompts for a group of writers, but you want so much more out of your life.

Look at the State of Me!: I can't stop eating decorative beads!

Salt Heart Press

"Invention, it must be humbly admitted, does not consist in creating out of void but out of chaos."

- Mary Shelley

We at Salt Heart Press seek the best in horror. We live for it, we crave it, we desire it — nothing gives us more pleasure than the thrills and chills found in the perfectly crafted dark tale. As such, it is our mission to seek out fresh voices in the genre, search out the new and unique, the brave and challenging. We want to be scared. We want to be haunted. And we want the same for you.

So take a look at the books we have and keep an eye out for those to come.

https://www.saltheartpress.com/

Check out these other spooky books from Salt Heart Press

What Remains When The Stars Burn Out
a horror collection by P.L. McMillan

If Only a Heart and other tales of terror
by Caleb Stephens

Confirmed Sightings: a triple cryptid creature feature
featuring Bridget D. Brave, P.L. McMillan, and Ryan Marie Ketterer

The Darkness Beyond The Stars: an anthology of space horror
edited by P.L. McMillan

Welcome To Your Body: Lessons in Evisceration
edited by Ryan Marie Ketterer

between doorways: explorations into liminal space
edited by TJ Price

Sisters of the Crimson Vine
by P.L. McMillan

The White Horse
by Rebecca Harrison

Portraits of Decay
by Carson Winter

www.ingramcontent.com/pod-product-compliance
Lightning Source LLC
LaVergne TN
LVHW010658110826
845149LV00014B/3145
* 9 7 9 8 9 9 2 5 9 0 0 9 8 *